FRIGHT NIGHT

A novel by John Skipp & Craig Spector
Based on the screenplay by Tom Holland

Copyright © 1985
Columbia Pictures Industries, Inc.
All Rights Reserved.

The characters and events in this book are fictitious.
Any similarity to real persons, living, dead or undead
is coincidental and not intended by the author.

No part of this book may be reproduced in any form
or by any electronic or mechanical means, including
information storage and retrieval systems, without
permission in writing from the publisher, except by a
reviewer who may quote brief passages in a review.

Encyclopocalypse Publications
www.encyclopocalypse.com

Contents

One	5
Two	17
Three	21
Four	27
Five	31
Six	35
Seven	43
Eight	51
Nine	55
Ten	61
Eleven	73
Twelve	77
Thirteen	87
Fourteen	95
Fifteen	99
Sixteen	107
Seventeen	113
Eighteen	123
Nineteen	129
Twenty	139
Twenty-One	143
Twenty-Two	149
Twenty-Three	153
Twenty-Four	159
Twenty-Five	165
Twenty-Six	171
Twenty-Seven	179
Twenty-Eight	183
Epilogue	191

One

Charley Brewster wasn't sure where the inspiration behind bra clasps came from. If God were responsible, then clearly he wasn't meant to fondle Amy's naked breasts, in which case he should feel guilty as hell. If, on the other hand, the devil were behind it, then God clearly approved of bared-bosom explorations, in which case it was his sacred duty to go about it with all speed.

Charley gave this weighty philosophical question a full second of his undivided attention. Then he went back to struggling, sneakily, with the goddam clasps. *Whoever* was behind it had done an impressive job. Breaking into Amy's treasure chest was harder than breaking into Evil Ed's gym locker.

And Amy wasn't making it any easier. She clearly believed that God had secured her bra tightly around her for a reason. One tiny chunk of his brain could sympathize: she was simply being stronger, and more righteous, than he. The rest of him wished that she would just cut it out, because he wanted Amy Peterson so bad that it hurt.

They were grappling on the floor next to Charley's bed, a couple of throw pillows cushioning their heads and shoulders. Charley was slightly on top, a half-hearted attempt at the dominant male position. She wouldn't let him mount her completely. Her hips had ground against his at one point, however—he was *sure* of it—and the one overriding thought in his head was, *If I do this right, I'm gonna make it, gonna make it, gonna...*

His right hand swept nonchalantly along her naked back. She tensed as it neared those hateful hooks. He veered to the left, moving up to take her shoulder beneath the buttoned blouse. *You're not fooling anyone, you know,* he could almost hear her thinking.

Throughout it all, they continued to kiss: tongues describing loop-dee-loops, lips nearly spot-welded together. If she didn't want him to go any further, she also didn't want him to stop. Her hands were under his shirt as well, and he noticed that they'd hit *his* nipples a couple of times without being struck by lightning.

Dammit, this is stupid, he silently muttered. Then Amy did something particularly nice with her mouth, and he lost himself in the kiss for a minute.

Self-consciousness returned with the soundtrack music. Spooky strings— foreboding, swelling—in accompaniment to the stilted dialogue from the three-inch speaker of his portable TV:

"Oh, darling." Young, male, slightly effeminate, British. "Darling, darling, darling. I can't tell you how frightfully much I've missed you."

"Yes, Jonathan." Young, female, also British, with the cool and cheesy theatrical creepiness of the living dead, *circa* 1945. "It's so marvelous to see you again."

"You are so beautiful tonight, my love. Your skin, so soft and white. Your lips, so red and..."

"Yes?" A short pause. Then, wickedly, "Would you like to kiss them?"

The music reared its corny head, melodramatically mounting in intensity. *Jesus,* Charley thought, lips still grinding on Amy's. The movie made him feel suddenly ridiculous, his clownish insecurities blown up to the size of floats in the Macy's Thanksgiving Day Parade. *They probably aren't even opening their mouths,* he added sourly. *It's stuff like this that makes us so hung up.*

He steeled himself for a moment, then decided

to go for broke. Amy wriggled beneath him as he went for her bra clasp with both hands. Her hands grabbed him just below the armpits and tried to push him away. He held on tenaciously, arms wrapped around her, desperately wrenching at the miserable elastic. The hooks held tight. He began to suspect that she'd glued them closed. She was beating on his back now. There was no time to lose. Charley made one frantic last-ditch effort, and—

"STOP, O CREATURE OF THE NIGHT!"

The voice was deep and commanding. It was also coming from the TV set. Charley responded to it anyway, freezing just long enough for Amy to successfully push him away.

On the screen, the vampire hissed.

"God damn it," Charley moaned, and his gaze flickered over to the screen. The beautiful vampire woman was backing away from Peter Vincent, teeth bared. The fearless vampire hunter advanced, a wooden stake in one hand and a prodigious mallet in the other.

"I've come for you," the hero said.

Peter Vincent was tall and foreboding, his gaunt features taut beneath his stovepipe hat. Everything about him was dire and sober, from his black suit and cape to the smoldering darkness of his eyes.

Amy Peterson, on the other hand, was cute and cuddly. She had a wholesome face and a wanton body; they mirrored the conflict in her soul. When she looked at him, bright-eyed and cheerleader-pretty, he was struck with the full brunt of teenage love and adulation; when she touched him, every nerve in his body screamed with lust.

She refused to look at him, so Charley turned back to the movie. The music was really howling now, and the vampire shrieked as the stake pounded home. There was a little blood at the corners of her mouth, and her eyes were wild.

"I'm sorry," Amy said from behind him.

"Yeah," Charley mumbled, his eyes pasted to

the screen. "I really am."

"Yeah, I know. I bet." He knew he was being pissy. There was something perversely satisfying about it. A minute ago, he'd been physically pleading with her. If she had to crawl a little now, well... that might just bwake his widdow heart.

"Oh, Charley, cut it out. And don't be mad at me, either. I can't help it."

"You can't help it," Charley echoed sarcastically. He thumped his fist against the shag carpet for effect, then leapt to his feet and started pacing around the room. "Well, what am I supposed to do about it? I can't help it, either! We've been going together for almost a year—"

"Three months," she corrected quietly.

"Well, almost *half* a year, then—" he stormed on, inconsolable "—and all I ever hear is 'Charley, stop it' and 'I'm sorry!' It's making me crazy. It really is."

He'd never yelled at her like that before, and it made him a little uncomfortable. He stopped in front of the window and looked from Amy to the screen.

The words *Fright Night* appeared in big dripping letters, the Channel 13 logo below it.

Then a Carvel Ice Cream commercial came on, and Charley turned to face his ghostly windowpane reflection.

While the gravelly voice droned on about Cookie Puss, Charley appraised himself. *Yeah, you're a real Cookie Puss, all right*, he thought bitterly. *You're as plain as a bag of potatoes.*

In truth, Charley Brewster was not a bad-looking guy. He wasn't exactly rugged, but there was nothing cutesie about him, either. He was just a solid, decent-looking kid: brown hair, brown eyes, a prominent Roman nose, full lips and symmetrical ears on a pleasant, rounded face. Nothing special, but nothing to kick out of bed.

When the commercial switched to an ad for the Rancho Corvallis Dragway (the Woody Woodpecker voice howling, "SATURDAY! SATURDAY!"), Amy snuck up behind him and snaked her arms around his neck.

"I'm really sorry," she purred, and then nailed him with an entirely believable kiss. It lasted through the spots for Slim Whitman and Barney's Karpet Kingdom, then cut off with the Planned Parenthood ad.

When they pulled apart, Amy stared at a spot on his shoulder. She was blushing, and her features were set in a kind of startled determination.

"Would you like to make love to me?" she tried to say. It came out as little more than a whisper.

Charley was stunned. A lump the size of his thumb got lodged in his throat. "Are you serious?" he croaked.

She nodded, red-faced and strangely resolute. She still couldn't look him in the eyes; when he leaned down to kiss her, she turned her face up to his with her eyes already closed.

Charley's heart and hormones were doing elaborate backflips. His erection which had softened, sprang back to attention. They turned slowly in each other's arms as they kissed, and for some reason he kept his eyes open, vision gliding along the wall, turning into the room, sweeping over the *Fright Night* logo on the tube...

...and then riveting on a spot in the darkness beyond the window.

What the hell? he thought, lips disengaging from Amy's. He couldn't believe what he was seeing.

Amy slipped out of Charley's grasp and slid gracefully over to the bed. Part of her felt incredibly awkward: the frightened virgin before the blood and pain gave way to what she hoped would be ecstasy. But she had made a decision, and the choosing made her stronger somehow. Her movements betrayed none of her insecurity.

I'm going to do it, she thought. *I'm really going to do it*. She flopped down on the black-and-white comforter that covered the bed, coyly seductive, and looked at her chosen first lover.

He was staring out the window. In fact, he had grabbed the binoculars off his desk and was using them to get a closer look. She thought it was a little bit strange, but she was too engrossed in her own feelings to bend too far out of shape.

Peter Vincent came back on the tube just as Amy began to unbutton her blouse. This Peter Vincent was a good twenty years older than the one in the movie: his jet-black hair now turned gray, his strong and handsome face lined with age and pitted with weariness. His delivery was stale as ever, but the air of certain victory he'd brought into his films had been replaced by an aura of defeat. In his gaudy cloak and rumpled black suit, he looked like a vampire who'd switched from blood to Geritol.

"I hope you are enjoying our *Fright Night* feature, *Blood Castle*," he intoned, mock-sinister. Behind him, Styrofoam tombstones wobbled on a cheesy television soundstage; a crudely drawn full-moon-over-the-cemetery mural dangled crookedly from a pair of visible wires. "It's an all-time favorite monster marathon of mine..."

Amy stopped listening. She was down to her last two buttons, and Charley still hadn't turned around. *Maybe he's just being shy*, she thought, but it didn't quite ring true. For one thing, he hadn't been the least bit shy about pawing her like an animal; for another, he still had the binoculars pasted to his head.

If he wanted to see something up close, she reasoned, one would think he'd be aiming them at her tits.

"Charley, I'm ready," she said, very softly. He didn't respond. She tried it again, a little more loudly.

No response. A bit annoyed, and more than a bit confused, she said, "Charley!" once more.

"Amy," he said suddenly. "You're not going to believe this, but there are two guys carrying a coffin into the house next door."

Two guys—Peter Vincent and Jonathan the wimp—were carrying a coffin on the TV screen. *Blood Castle* had resumed. "If you come here, you can see the exact same thing," she said, smiling wickedly. "With a couple of fringe benefits besides."

"Amy, I'm serious."

"So am I."

"No, you don't understand. They're... Jesus, they're carrying it into the cellar, through the storm doors." He sounded genuinely agitated.

He wasn't the only one. She was getting impatient, and goosebumps were starting to form on her exposed flesh. "Charley, cut it out and come here. I'm getting cold."

His only response was a muttered "Jesus," and a slight shift of position at the window.

"Charley," she growled, "do you want me or not?"

"Amy, come here and look at this," he said. It was as if she hadn't spoken. "Honest to God, this is weird—"

"Okay, that's *it!*" she yelled, rolling furiously off the bed, her feet thudding loudly on the floor. She fumbled with her buttons as she stomped toward the door. Charley finally turned around.

"You're a real jerk, Charley," she hissed at him, eyes flashing. "Just forget I ever offered. Just forget," and she waggled her finger for emphasis, "that you ever even knew me at all."

"But... but..." Charley was positively stymied. His jaw hung open; the binoculars were clutched dumbly in his hands. "Where are you going?"

"Away from you," she snapped, grabbing the doorknob and twisting it savagely. The door flew open with a thunderous bang as she stormed past it and down the hallway to the stairs.

All the desire had leaked right out of her like air from a ruptured balloon. The rage that took its place was white-hot and deadly. She hoped that Charley wouldn't be stupid enough to try to face it. She would singe the hair right out of his nostrils.

But he was coming, sure enough: clomping down the hallway after her, braying her name like a snotty-nosed toddler. She finished buttoning her blouse and hit the stairs noisily, hoping the clatter would wake his mother up and that he'd get in trouble.

"Amy, please!" he cried. She could hear him racing to catch up with her. "You gotta believe me! Those people were doing something really strange..."

"You're the only strange one around here, Charley." Her voice was level and full of venom. She refused to stop, or to look at him.

"But they were carrying a coffin!" He caught up with her at last, put one hand on her shoulder.

"*So what!*" she yelled, whirling to face him. He backed off, startled. It pleased her. "Listen, if you're so interested in coffins, why don't you just go over there and help them carry it? Better yet, why don't you go back up to your stupid Peter Vincent? *He's* probably still dragging one around!"

"He's *not* stupid," Charley countered. She'd hit a nerve, making fun of his hero. *Tough*, she thought, smiling through her anger.

"Tell you what," she concluded. "Here's the best idea yet. Why don't you just dig a nice deep hole and lay in it? Maybe the neighbors will let you borrow *their* coffin!"

"Amy!"

They hit the bottom of the stairs together, Amy striding quickly toward the living room and front door. Charley dragged slightly behind, which suited her splendidly, because it meant that she didn't have to look at his face. "I can show myself out—" she began.

And then a voice from the living room jarred her to a halt.

"Amy? Charley?" the voice called, chirping musically in the upper registers. "Is anything wrong?"

It was Mrs. Brewster, sitting smack dab in the middle of the living room, right in front of the TV. Her back was to them, but they could see her clearly. Amy frantically straightened clothes and hair, heard Charley doing the same. She felt suddenly stupid and mean.

"Are you two having a lovers' quarrel?" Mrs. Brewster pried sweetly.

"No, Mom. Nothing like that." Charley stepped past Amy and into the living room. He looked embarrassed. She felt a sudden rush of empathy for

12

him.

"Well, there's nothing wrong with a little spat now and then," Mrs. Brewster said, turning to face them. "I just read this article in *McCall's* today. It said that the divorce rate is seventy-eight per cent higher among couples who don't argue before marriage." She seemed to think it was a pretty impressive statistic.

"Mom, we're in high school." Charley's voice was plaintive.

"Well, yes, that's true." She looked puzzled for a moment, then brightened. "But it pays to plan ahead!"

Amy liked Mrs. Brewster. She was a classic Momicon: the kind of pretty-faced housewife on afternoon television who buys St. Joseph's aspirin for her children. Petite, in her mid-forties, with frosty-blond hair and a face that rarely failed to smile. She was terribly sweet and more than slightly dizzy... more than a little bit like her son.

She'd make a wonderful mother-in-law, Amy found herself thinking, and quickly stifled the thought.

"Amy?" Mrs. Brewster said. "Say hello to your mother for me, will you? And remind her that we're playing bridge at her house this weekend. I'll bring the Cheese Doodles if she makes her pecan pie." She giggled; Becky Peterson's pecan pie was legend.

"I certainly will," Amy said.

"Thank you, sweetie. You're a doll." They beamed at each other. *How can she possibly be so NICE?* Amy thought. Then Mrs. Brewster added, "And thank you for helping Charley with his algebra. It drives him crazy, poor dear. He just can't seem to get the hang of it. You know, I *always* had a hard time with math in school!"

She giggled. Amy could picture her, giggling her way through finals back in the fifties; she wondered what it would have been like to be a teenager then, and couldn't imagine it.

She wondered, briefly, what Mr. Brewster had been like. And why he'd left her.

Mrs. Brewster was prattling on about her

youth, her grades, some crazy girlfriend who was in love with Wally Cleaver. Amy shifted her attention to Charley for a second, wondering if she was still mad at him or not, wondering what *he* was feeling.

He was looking out the goddam window again.

She followed his gaze. From where she was standing, she couldn't see anything. If he was bored it was understandable, but it was not polite. *The least you could do is pretend to pay attention,* she told him silently.

She was pissed again. She tried not to let Mrs. Brewster see it. "Well, I've got to be running," she said. "I promised I'd be home by midnight, and I'm already a little late."

"Oh! Well, good night! And be careful going home. Drunk drivers are everywhere." Even when she was serious, the lines in Mrs. Brewster's face were smiling. Long-standing habit, immortalized in flesh.

"I'll be careful," Amy said. Then, almost as an afterthought, she turned to the window and said, "Good night, Charley."

"Yeah. Good night," he muttered, abstracted.

It was the last straw. She'd gone up and down and up and down with him; and even after she'd told him how she felt, he was still the same jerk, his binoculars pointing the wrong way.

He didn't turn until she'd slammed the door behind her.

"That wasn't very nice," Mrs. Brewster said, "not walking Amy to the door."

"What?" Charley said. His mind was aswirl. There were lights on in the house next door. He hadn't seen lights there for almost a year.

"It wasn't very nice. It was rude. You know that."

"Yeah, but..." There was no arguing with it. She was right. It *was* rude.

But the fact was that he had seen two strange men carry a coffin into the basement of an abandoned house. Now there were lights on in the living room. It seemed to him that Amy should have checked it out with him instead of just getting pissed. It seemed to him like he wasn't entirely off the wall in wanting to know just what the hell was going on.

"Mom," he said, "there are some people next door."

"Oh! That must be the new owner!"

"*What* new owner?"

"Didn't I tell you? Bob Hopkins finally sold the place."

"To who?"

"I don't know. Some man who likes to fix up old houses, apparently. I just hope that he knows what he's in for. That place would need a lot of work before *I'd* be willing to live there!"

She giggled. Mom always giggled. Sometimes he wanted to throttle her for it; sometimes it endeared her to him. Tonight it was completely irrelevant.

When he closed his eyes, he could still see the coffin: huge, ornate and bound in brass. It was a beautiful piece of work, and it looked incredibly old. It was the kind of thing that he would covet, ordinarily; the kind of thing that he and Evil Ed would have a blast with, camping it up in classic Peter Vincent style.

So why had he gotten such a horrible chill, seeing it? And why wouldn't the thought of it leave him alone?

As if in answer, the late-night newscaster came on TV: pudgy-faced and leisure-suited, the words "Robert Rodale" in videotype across his chest. "Good evening," he said. "This is a KTOR News Break. Tonight the headless body of an unidentified man was found behind the Rancho Corvallis railway station..."

Reflexively, Charley turned back to the window. The blinds were drawn in the house next door.

And the horror was only beginning.

Two

Fifth period ended at the sound of the bell, flooding the halls of Christopher L. Cushing High with life. Students swarmed through opening doors, running the maze of corridors from classroom to classroom like laboratory rats in search of Velveeta Heaven.

The exodus from Room 234 was slightly more lethargic than average. This was the room of the infamous Mr. Lorre: master of the pop quiz, inventor of the ten-ton homework assignment. He had sprung both on his Algebra II class today, and his victims were less than elated.

Charley Brewster dragged himself out of the classroom like a man crawling out of a train wreck. His quiz paper dangled limp from one hand. A large red "F" adorned it like the mark of the devil.

"The bastard," he moaned. "Why didn't he warn us?"

"That's the whole point of a pop quiz, Brewster. To surprise you."

Charley turned without enthusiasm to face the voice from behind him. Evil Ed Thompson was not the most heartwarming sight in the world, even at the best of times. And this was not one of them.

Evil Ed was a certified freako. He was short and spidery, with a Billy Idol hairdo and a rubbery face that could leer and twist itself in a million lunatic ways.

He was gloating now, and the smirk on his face would have made Jack Nicholson proud.

Evil Ed, of course, had aced the quiz. He always did. He was smart as a fucking whip. It was what let him get away with being so incredibly weird. It was also the key to his popularity, which was nil.

In fact, Charley was one of the few people who would talk with Ed Thompson at all. Sometimes Charley wondered why he bothered. The answer was obvious: they were the only two hard-core monster freaks in Cushing High.

"Cheer up, Bunky. You can always get your diploma off a matchbook, worse comes to worst."

"Piss off, Evil. You're a pain in the butt."

"Call me anything you want to, Boss. Only you're the one who's flunking algebra, not me."

Charley was trying to think of something snappy to come back with when something beautiful caught the periphery of his vision. He whirled to see Amy, nose in the air, schoolbooks cradled to her bosom as she marched past the doorway.

"Amy!" he called, brightening suddenly.

She brushed him off. He knew that she'd heard him. He knew that she knew that he knew that she'd heard him. The repercussions echoed back at him like a ricocheting bullet. He sagged further into his sneakers and leaned against the doorway as she disappeared into the crowd.

"What's the matter?" Evil Ed said, cackling. "She finally find out what you're really like?"

"Shut up, Eddie! I'm serious!"

"OOOO! OOOO!" Evil Ed made a grand display of flapping his wrists. "I'm rigid with terror, Chucko! I'm soiling my dydees!"

"Asshole!" Charley yelled, storming off in Amy's direction. She hadn't spoken to him since Saturday night, and he was deeply afraid that she never would again. He knew that he would never catch her—he was going to be late for sixth period, no matter how he looked at it—but some gut-level impetus made him follow her anyway, pointlessly, digging himself deeper as he went.

Behind him, Evil Ed's high-pitched cackle cut through the crowd. For some reason, it gave him a chill.

He'd been having a lot of them lately.

Three

Charley's beet-red sixty-eight Mustang wheeled into the driveway at dusk. He'd been driving aimlessly for the last two hours, radio cranking while he tried to air out his mind. It was getting weird in there, and he had reached the point where he needed to start sorting it out.

He needed to apologize to Amy, for one thing. He didn't quite know how to go about it—biting the big one wasn't one of his favorite pastimes—but he knew that it had to be done. There weren't words to express how much he missed her, how big an emptiness had formed inside as a result of her not being around. The flip side of love was rearing its ugly head for the first time. He didn't just *want* to see her; he *needed* to see her, with every fiber in his being. And he needed to concoct a scheme that would bring them back together, no matter how low into the dirt he had to grovel.

That was for starters.

Then there was the house next door. He had to straighten himself out in terms of that coffin business. He had seen it, yes; it was a strange thing to own, yes again. But then, as he'd noted before, it was something he'd pick up in a second if he had the bucks. It was a pretty cool thing to own. Maybe, if he screwed his balls on, he might drop by and visit neighbors quirky enough to invest in things like that.

Schoolwork came in at a big Number Three. It was obvious that he had some work to do if he didn't want to repeat the year. It wasn't that he was too stupid to understand; it was just that he generally didn't give a shit.

But he didn't want to spend another year in eleventh grade while all his friends plunged forward into their last year of school. He didn't want a reputation as a full-blown airhead. Whether he liked it or not—whether it made *sense* or not—he would have to get cracking and learn what they wanted him to know.

Algebra was the big one. Algebra was the first one that he had to tackle. *And if I get it down,* he thought, *Amy will really be impressed. She'll come over to help me and I'll already know what I'm doing. She'll be shocked. Maybe she'll faint, and I can get her undressed before she has time to argue.* He didn't know what he'd missed on Saturday night. He'd never seen her open blouse.

Charley put the car in park and cut the engine, sighing heavily. Mom would want to know why he was late, and he'd have to make up something. It wasn't that she was bitchy; it was just that she felt like she needed to know every tiny little thing that happened in his life. He wondered if every mother in the world was like that.

A cab rounded the corner onto King Street just as he got out of the car. It was surprising, because cabs almost never came into his neighborhood. Rancho Corvallis was an automotive town; the bus service stank, and the one cab company had maybe six cars. Charley paused to watch the anomaly cruise toward him. He was startled when it stopped in front of his house.

He was even more startled when the foxiest girl he had ever seen slid out of the cab and faced him.

She was blond and blue-eyed and incredibly gorgeous. She had a body that could cause cardiac arrest in one-celled organisms, packed into a dress that clung to her every curve as if its life depended on it. When she smiled at him, Charley felt his knees turn to molten butter.

22

"Is this Ninety-nine King?" she asked, going into a Little Girl Lost act. The sight of her sexy, pouting lips sent his hormones into overdrive.

"Uh-bubba," he said. She looked at him quizzically. She didn't understand that he was trying to get his mouth to work. "Uh, n-no," he continued. "It's r-right next d-door." He pointed a jittering finger.

"Thanks," she purred, smiling. The effect was devastating. Somehow he sensed that she knew what she was doing to him. Even as she turned away, offering a spectacular view from the rear, he realized that part of him went with her—wrapped around her little finger, as it were.

Charley whistled softly, appreciatively, as she departed. She smiled back at him, over her shoulder. She'd heard it. He blushed a little, but couldn't keep himself from smiling back.

Wonder if she'll be a regular fixture around here, he mused. He hoped she would, though it might not endear him to his new neighbor. *Whoever he is*, Charley added, *he's got excellent taste.*

Lucky bastard.

He watched her walk up to the old house and put a dainty finger to the buzzer. The door opened almost immediately. Charley couldn't see who let her in. But she was still smiling as she disappeared into the house. It washed away whatever nervousness he had.

All was right with the world.

Several hours into the darkness of that night, Charley wandered down to the kitchen for some Cheese Doodles and Coke. Mom was at the table, blearily reading the evening paper. She'd worked all day, and he knew that she would not last much longer into the night.

Lights were on in the old house. He thought about the girl again, peered over for a glimpse of her through the windows. All the blinds were drawn. *Oh, well*, he thought, turning absently to his mother.

"Mom, have you seen the new guy next door yet?"

"No," she said yawning. "But I've heard a couple of things."

"Like what?"

"Well, his name is Jerry Dandrige. He's a young man, and I hear that he's very attractive." She giggled and yawned at the same time, no mean feat. "I also hear that he's got a live-in carpenter. With my luck, they're probably gay."

Charley grinned and wrinkled his forehead. "No," he said. "I don't think so."

"Oh? What do you know that I don't?" She leaned forward in her chair, almost hungrily.

"Oh, nothing." He opened the fridge and pulled a can of Coke off the plastic six-pack ring. A quick scan of the counter revealed an absence of Cheese Doodles. "Are we all out of munchies?"

"'Fraid so." Pause. "So what do you know about Jerry Dandrige?"

"Nothing. I told you."

"I think you're..." yawn "... holding out on me."

"No, I'm not. Honest." He let the refrigerator swing shut and headed for the living room. "Look, I gotta go up and study some more, okay?"

"You're *studying?*" She sounded genuinely shocked.

"What do you think I've been doing for the last couple of hours?" he called back over his shoulder. Then he was climbing the stairs to his room, her response muffled and unintelligible.

It was true, though. He'd been at it since dinner. His desk was a clutter of textbooks and notebooks: English III and American government, geography and the dreaded algebra. There was a lot of back homework that had never been done, more than enough to keep him busy all night.

Most of the easiest stuff had been dispensed with already. He was down to brass tacks, and it was driving him crazy. He sat down and looked at the open algebra book. Its contents made him want to scream.

24

It is essential for you to memorize this rule: *The square of the sum of two terms is equal to the square of the first term, plus twice the product of the first term by the second term, plus the square of the second term.*

"Right," he muttered. It had lost him on the first curlicue of logic. He looked at the equation that was supposed to illustrate the point.

$$(a+b)2 = a2 + 2ab + b2$$

"Yeah, okay." It sort of seemed to make sense when you looked at the numbers, although he couldn't say exactly how. The explanation was still total gibberish to him.

Charley popped open the Coke and swigged heavily on it. If someone'd offered him a beer, he would have drained it in one gulp. *They want me to memorize this shit*, he silently moaned, *and I can't even figure out what they're talking about.*

He was locked in mid-swallow when the scream slashed a hole in the night.

Carbonated sugar-water sprayed through the air, spattering the desktop, books and papers with a million wet splotches of brown. He choked, the bubbles scorching his nostrils, burning like fire in his spasming throat. Tears flooded his eyes. He cupped his whole unhappy face with his hands.

By the time he recovered, the scream was long gone. It had only lasted a second, if that, and it had almost been faint enough to write off as imagination.

But it was still ringing in his mind's ear; a single bright bauble of terrified sound, one second of horror that twitched in the air.

And then silence.

Total, terrible silence.

Charley looked out the window. All the lights were off at the Dandrige house. Its walls were blanketed in darkness. He didn't know for a fact that the scream had come from there.

But when he pictured the beautiful girl in his mind, it was no longer a heartwarming recollection. Her face and the scream were inextricably locked together.

He doubted that he would see or hear either of them again.

His algebra homework was still spread out before him. He marveled at how much the drops of cola looked like blood.

Four

Charley sat in his usual booth at Wally's, blearily rubbing his forehead. An open-faced Wallyburger sat expectantly before him, awaiting its customary overdose of mustard, ketchup and garlic powder.

Charley was oblivious. To the burger. To the half dozen video games screeching and squonking in the background. To their players, smoking and laughing and absorbing the latest in recreational radiation. To the garbled din of "The Young and the Restless" blasting from the Trinitron bolted to the wall and aimed right at him.

The nonstop chaos that formed the daily fabric of Wally's Burger Heaven, teen mecca of the Rancho Corvallis Mall, was all but lost on Charley. He wanted nothing more than to continue massaging his face, as if the act might magically revitalize his beleaguered brain.

"My day was a disaster," he moaned. "My *life* is a disaster..."

The burger sat, mutely sympathetic. He slathered it with condiments apathetically.

The unfairness of it all was entirely beyond him. *Stay up all night studying, then fall asleep in Lorre's class. Way to go, Brewster. What a chump. You'll be in summer school the rest of your stupid life.*

The thought made his stomach twist into hard little knots. He stared at the burger, then swept it aside. His life was ruined, utterly ruined.

"Amy hates me," he mumbled. The words stuck in his throat like a lump of sour milk. Three months of heartfelt emotion and raw animal cunning, right down the dumper. *She'll never go to bed with me now. Hell, she won't even speak to me!*

He wondered if Peter Vincent had such female troubles.

No, he thought. *Peter Vincent doesn't have troubles like this. Peter Vincent doesn't get all wet behind the ears about some creepy guy's coffin, either. Peter Vincent would stake a vampire with one hand while groping some bleached-blond fraulein with tits the size of basketballs in the other.*

He was so engrossed in thoughts of Peter Vincent that Amy slid into the booth beside him without his realizing it. She watched him for a moment, his hands threatening to dig ruts in his forehead. Obviously lost in despair.

Her heart quivered a little. She put on her best sweetie-pie voice and purred, "Hi, Charley..."

No reply. Probably lost without her. She resumed, undaunted.

"*Hi*, Charley..."

Charley looked up. His eyes focused and widened in surprise. "Amy?" Then, recovering somewhat, "Amy! Look, I'm really sorry about the other night. I'm such a putz. I—"

"It was my fault, not yours," she said, all sweetness.

"It was?" This was not the expected response. He looked like a man who'd been slugged with a sockful of nickels.

"Uh-huh..." she nodded, all seduction. She touched his hand lightly.

Charley felt faint. If God Almighty Himself had descended from heaven and sprayed him with a seltzer bottle, he'd have been no less surprised. *This is it*, he thought.

He squeezed her hand. "Look, Amy. I love you. I'm sorry about the other night, and I never want to fight with you again. Okay?"

Amy leaned back in the booth and beamed. "God, I'm so glad we're getting this whole mess straightened out. I've been really miserable these last few days, Charley, and I..." She faltered, eyes shifting to the table top. "... I'd kinda like to pick up where we left off. Tonight, maybe?"

No response.

"Charley?" She looked up, smiling.

Her smile froze on her face as she realized that Charley was gone, halfway across Wally's toward the TV on the wall.

"Charley, are you listening to me?"

Charley wasn't listening to anybody. Charley felt as if his entire consciousness had been stuffed into a cardboard tube and fired straight at the TV screen. The whole world—love, Amy, Wallyburgers, sex—all faded into a miasma of gray mush as Charley stared, transfixed by the four o'clock news.

Another murder. The victim's face, flashing on the screen.

A face that was all too familiar.

It's the fox. His mind reeled. *Omigod, I just saw her yesterday...*

... That scream...

His ears strained for the sound, caught it in mid-sentence.

"... police are searching for further clues in the mutilation-slaying of Cheryl Lane, a known prostitute who appears to be the latest victim of the 'Rancho Corvallis Killer.' Authorities are quick to point out that..."

"Know what I heard on the police band last night?"

Charley's attention snapped back. He turned to find Evil Ed standing beside him, leering like an idiot. Charley grimaced. "Knowing you, it must be bad."

Evil Ed grinned. "There've been two identical murders in the last two days, Brewster. And *get this*," he added gleefully. "Both of 'em had their *heads* cut off! Can you stand it?" He cackled. "Fuck *Fright Night*, Chucko. We got a *real* monster here!"

"You're a sick man, Evil. Real sick."

"Oh, Char-ley..." A voice from his past, coming up behind. Charley's blood froze.

"Amy?..." he began.

Charley wheeled around and caught a cold Wallyburger right in the kisser. Amy ground it in for good measure, sending gobs of condiments dripping out the sides onto his down vest. Evil Ed hastily got out of range, enjoying the spectacle immensely.

Amy finished grinding, let go of the mashed bun. It stayed right where she'd left it, plastered to his face like something from a Warner Brothers cartoon. She wheeled around and stomped off, royally pissed but triumphant.

"Amy..." Charley stood there, dripping rings of onion, looking absolutely ridiculous. The crowd cast furtive glances and giggled. Evil Ed sauntered up, cooing maternally and wiping away flecks of ground beef with a hankie.

"Oooooo, Brewster, you're *sooo* cool. You've got such a touch with the ladies..."

"Amy!" Charley shouted, but it was too late.

Amy was long gone.

30

Five

The Shelby Mustang whipped down the street and into the narrow driveway with practiced precision, hooking around the back of the Brewster house and sliding neatly into the garage. It cleared by inches the lawn mower and garden tools piled haphazardly against the side wall, and stopped just short of going clear through the back.

Charley threw it into park and killed the engine. He checked his reflection in the rear-view mirror; he'd washed his face pretty thoroughly, but there were still some telltale splotches of mustard and ketchup on his vest. That was all he needed right now: to explain to his mother. God...

He grabbed his books and started out of the garage. The neighbor's house loomed before him, as though waiting for some cue to stomp through the hedge, across the driveway and...

He shook his head. That was dumb. The house next door had been empty for years. Sure, it looked like your basic haunted house—he sometimes wondered if years of staring out his bedroom window at the place had warped his mind—but it had never before held such a sense of foreboding.

Until last night.

Until the scream.

Charley studied the side of the house: three stories high, Victorian, imposing. The largest house on the block, and the oldest. It had not aged gracefully, its elegance having long since given way to a paint-flecked and gloomy decrepitude.

Twice as big and ten times as ugly, as Evil Ed was fond of saying.

There was a squat, ill-kept hedge running the length of the driveway, neatly dividing the properties. The neighbor's lawn had grown wildly out of control where it hadn't died. Weeds choked the base of the house, partially obscuring the basement windows *(which you couldn't see through anyway, dammit!)*, the long-forgotten coal chute...

...and the storm doors.

Where they took the coffin.

Charley's feet were moving before his brain had told them, carrying him across the driveway before he had a chance to argue. Not that he would have put up much of a fight.

He *had* to know what was going on.

And there was only one way to do that.

(Fuck Fright Night, *Chucko. We got a real monster here!)*

He had left his books piled in the driveway and pushed his way through the hedge. The yard looked even worse from the other side. He cast a wary glance around, his own house looking like an oasis of cheerful suburbia, and crept toward the storm doors.

Charley climbed onto the doors and tried to peek in the windows. No such luck; there were curtains or blankets or something on every window on the first floor.

He jumped down and studied the storm doors. They were the big, heavy, steel lean-to type, very rugged and almost as old as the house itself. He grabbed the handle and gave it a tug.

No chance. There was a brand new cylinder lock installed. One of the fancy ones, a Fichet or something, the kind that folks who live in big cities might need. *But in this neighborhood?* he thought. *Nobody needs security like that around here.*

Unless they've got something to hide.

He was about to get on his knees and check out the basement windows when the voice stopped him dead in his tracks.

"Hey, kid! What the hell do you think you're doing?"

If he'd eaten lunch, he probably would've thrown up. The voice wasn't just stern; it wasn't just harsh. That voice was *cold:* the kind of voice that says *I've killed people for less than that* and means it most sincerely.

Charley put on his most casual face and turned around. He quickly wished he hadn't.

The source of the voice was, beyond any doubt, one of the coffin-carrying neighbors. He looked like a cross between Harrison Ford and Anthony Perkins: rugged, angular features and deep eyes under prominent eyebrows.

Those eyes. Cold. Incalculable. Any pretense to attractiveness ended with those eyes. He moved a little closer. Charley instinctively backed up, almost tripping over the storm doors. He was very close to panic, fumbling for an excuse.

"Ah, *n-n-nothing*," he stammered.

The man was dressed in work clothes, a carpenter's apron around his waist. He held a large claw hammer in his right hand, gesturing with it, dripping casual menace. He smiled; rather, his lips skinned back to reveal perfectly even teeth. There was no affection in it. His eyes remained unchanged.

"See that it stays that way, kid. Mr. Dandrige doesn't like unexpected guests.

Uh, yessir, you bet, no problem." Charley fumfuhed a few seconds more, trying like hell to be nonchalant when part of his brain kept screaming *don'tkillmedon'tkillmedon't...* He beat as graceful a retreat as possible, under the circumstances, cold sweat trickling down his back as he plowed through the hedge.

When he dared venture a look back, ever so casual as he stopped to retrieve his books, the man was gone. The house seemed just a little darker, more hulking, more... dead.

He hoped it was just his imagination.

Six

The Marine Corps Band pumped its last majestic chords, the Blue Angels arced in tight formation into the sunset, and Charley's head tipped back, mouth open in a full-throated snore.

Channel 13 signed off for the night. Flickering snow filled the TV screen—the only light in the room.

He was supposed to be on stakeout. He was not very good at it. No stamina. He had set it up well enough: lights out, a nice comfy chair, the binoculars and a well-stocked store of munchies. He was determined to know if anything funny was going to occur.

But after four hours of staring intently at the utterly black exterior of the neighbor's house, boredom and fatigue took their toll. Had he stayed awake, he would have seen the cab pull up and dispatch its lone passenger. Seen the stranger climb the steps next door, and the light flick on shortly thereafter.

The light in the window. Directly across from him.

Instead, Charley slept.
And he dreamed.

In his dream, there was music: haunting, sensual music that pulsed and strobed and seemed to go right through him. And voices: whispers that rustled like dry leaves, too quiet to understand. But relentless.

There was a presence in the room. Hot. Pulsing. The air was heavy with a musky odor.

He felt the woman's touch. Vibrant. Hungry. He groped blindly, found her belly, her breasts, her neck.

Her neck was beautiful.

He wanted her badly.

Brushing her hair back, he kissed her neck, rubbing his teeth along the cords of tight muscle, tasting her salt skin. He felt the need burning in him: to touch, to taste, to kiss...

He pulled her body closer. She turned to meet his gaze...

... and her eyes glowed, bright red and feral, the sockets sunken and shriveled, the flesh of her face puckered and ancient, mouth yawning wide to reveal plaque-encrusted teeth, long teeth, very, very sharp. Her nails dug into the small of his back, and...

Charley awoke with a start.

"What a weird dream," he mumbled, rubbing his eyes, disoriented. Then he heard the music.

It was coming from the window across the driveway. And there was light. He sat up, clutching his binoculars.

The shade was up, offering an unobstructed view of what was going on in the room. Charley's throat went dry. The music was coming from there.

Haunting, sensual music...

The window was open, the night breeze fluttered the curtains. A beautiful young woman stood in front of the window, rocking seductively in time with the music. Her blouse was open, exposing her midriff.

It was a very nice midriff. Charley swallowed hard and glued the binoculars to his eyes.

The woman was swaying even *more* sensually, if such a thing were possible. She stared into the middle distance, as if enthralled by something she saw there. Then, to Charley's complete amazement, she slid out of her blouse and stood still, torso glistening in the moonlight.

Charley rarely saw so much unabashedly nubile female flesh. He leaned over, slapped off the TV and enveloped himself in darkness, watching.

She was incredible: petite, with shoulder-length hair, full pouting lips and wonderful breasts. Charley bit his lip, hard. *Who is this guy?* he wondered. *How does he get these women?*

And what is he doing to them?

He was stumped. Still, she didn't appear to be in any danger. In fact, she seemed to be quite enjoying herself. She was rocking back and forth now, breasts jiggling languorously in her bra. She turned at one point and faced Charley directly. He ducked, afraid she'd see him.

But she didn't. He was sure of it. Something in her movements bewildered him; they were too fluid, too dreamy, too...

Drugged. The word came to him. *Or hypnotized. I don't know.* It scared him, suddenly, and he was half tempted to lean out the window and call to her.

Then Dandrige appeared.

The man was, in his own way, as beautiful as the girl. He crossed the room as if gliding several inches above the floor; and when he reached the girl, he seemed to hover more than stand. He touched her shoulders, and she seemed to stiffen with anticipation.

Dandrige massaged her shoulders tenderly for a moment, then reached around and deftly unhooked her bra with a grace and economy of motion that amazed Charley almost as much as the act itself.

The bra slid to the floor. Her nipples were hard. Dandrige cupped a breast in each hand. She arched back, lips parted.

Charley, meanwhile, was losing his mind. It was too cruel. His girlfriend hated him, he was failing algebra, and the neighbor was threatening him with terminal carpentry. Now *this* guy was rubbing the nubbins off the girl of his dreams.

The girl of his dreams...

He salt bolt upright in his chair. The girl in the window, the girl in Dandrige's arms...

37

... was the girl from his dream.

He looked out the window. Dandrige, one hand still cupping a breast, brushed the girl's hair away from the slope of her neck with the other. He kissed her neck, rubbing his teeth along the cords of taut muscle. Her eyes glazed over. Her lips moved, imperceptibly whispering, soft as the rustle of dry leaves. Dandrige smiled, showing teeth.

"Oh, no," Charley whimpered. "Oh, God, no..."

Dandrige's teeth were long and very very sharp. Charley gasped and dropped the binoculars. They hit the floor with a clatter.

Dandrige stopped, teeth poised an inch from her neck. Charley sank further into the darkness of his room, unable to look away. Dandrige seemed to be looking right at him. Right *through* him.

With eyes that were red as glowing coals.

Charley felt his bowels turn to water. "No..." he whispered.

Dandrige smiled. Long, yellow teeth.

He reached up, grasping the shade with long, crooked fingers. Pulled it down slowly, lackadaisically.

And waved bye-bye.

"*MOM!!!*" Charley bolted down the hall, hitting his mother's door loud and hard. "*MOM!!!*"

Judy Brewster was down for the count, lost in a Sominex-induced dreamland. A pink satin sleep mask effectively blotted out the entire upper half of her face. Charley's dramatic entrance barely served to prod her to consciousness. "Charley?" she asked blearily.

"You gotta wake *up*, Mom!" He was hysterical, his arms flying wildly around him. "I don't *believe* it! Mom! Jesus!"

Judy looked at her son as if he were an emissary from the planet Zontar. "What?" she asked sleepily. "What are you talking about?"

"He has *fangs*, Mom! The guy who bought the house has *fangs*!"

"Charley..."

"I'm SERIOUS!" His voice squeaked into dog-annoying frequencies. He made an effort to bring it back down. "I saw him through the window with my binoculars, Mom! He's got *fangs*, I tell you!"

"Binoculars? Charley, that's *spying!* That's not nice."

"*FANGS, Mother! LONG ones!*"

"Oh, Charley." She yawned heavily and rolled over. "I have to be at work at seven tomorrow."

Charley stared at his mother, incredulous. He was about to try a more subtle approach, like throttling her, when a car door slammed outside. Leaping to the window, he saw the handyman walking away from a shiny black Cherokee Jeep. Its gate was down, as if in anticipation of a heavy load.

"*Argh!*" Charley was out of his mother's bedroom as quickly as he'd entered.

Judy sat up in bed. "Charley?" she said.

Charley slipped out the back door and scuttled across the driveway toward the hedge. The rear door of the Dandrige house was wide open, the porch light providing the only illumination.

His heart was pounding, sending blood surging into his temples. Fatigue, exertion and terror mingled inside him, making him light-headed. He crouched down in the bushes, feeling ill.

The handyman came out the back door, carrying a large bundle wrapped in plastic and trussed with heavy twine. A gaping hole opened in the pit of his stomach as Charley guessed its nature.

The handyman tossed the bag unceremoniously into the cargo hold of the Jeep. He was about to climb in, and Charley was about to get sick, when the flutter of leathery wings froze them both.

Charley looked around, afraid to move, afraid to breathe.

The beating wings ended in a flurry of motion to his left. He scanned the darkened façade of the Dandrige house, searching for its source.

39

Less than ten feet away, the night air seemed to darken, to condense, into the shape of a man. The specter solidified and moved across the lawn. Toward the Jeep.

"Here. You forgot something."

It was Dandrige. He tossed his servant a purse.

The bundle's purse.

The man caught it one-handed, turned back to the Jeep with a nod.

Charley was stifling a scream in the bushes when a shaft of light cut through the darkness behind him. He hunkered down, fearing the inevitable.

"Charley? Char-ley?"

Thanks, Mom.

He was terrified. The man and the shadow froze. They wheeled around, searching the blackness for his presence. Dandrige actually took a couple of steps in his direction.

Charley jumped up and ran for his life, back to Mom, apple pie and anything else he could pile in the way. He disappeared into the relative safety of his kitchen.

"Little bastard," hissed the handyman, starting after him. He was restrained by Dandrige, who held his other hand up in a gesture of patience.

"Billy," said the master with a gracious smile. "There'll be plenty of time for that later.

"Plenty of time."

Judy busied herself around the kitchen, more out of habit than anything else. She looked at her son. *Poor baby. He's been studying too much.*

"Here, honey. Have some cocoa."

"Mom, I don't *need* any cocoa! I didn't *have* a nightmare! I'm telling you those guys *killed* a girl tonight!"

Judy felt his forehead, checking for fever. He was cool to the touch. *Maybe something he ate?*

40

"MOM! I'm *not* sick!" Charley pushed her hand away. "The guy *did* have fangs! A bat *did* fly over my head! Dandrige *did* step out of the shadows!" He was pissed. "You know what that means, don't you?"

Judy stared at him worriedly. "What, dear?"

"He's a VAMPIRE!"

Seven

"A *what?*" Amy's face, at that moment, looked an awful lot like his mother's.

"A *vampire*, dammit! Haven't you listened to anything I said?"

"Charley," she said. Her voice was flat and slightly forlorn. "This is really childish, do you know that? This is a really dumb way to try and get me back."

"Forget it," Charley fumed, turning for the door. "I'm going to the police."

They were in Amy's kitchen, on a sunny and cheerful afternoon. The room was spacious and clean, brightly painted, flooded with light from the huge bay windows. It was an unlikely spot for a major confrontation, but that didn't make a bit of difference.

"Charley, this is crazy!"

"Tell me about it." His voice was blunt as a truncheon.

Amy ran in front of him and blocked the door. Her expression had turned desperate. Her hands clamped onto his shoulders as she looked him straight in the eye.

"Charley. Stop. Listen," she said. He stopped and listened, but the expression on his face said that he wasn't really hearing. "You can't go to the police with a story like that," she continued. "They'll lock you up. I'm serious."

"All right, all right. I won't say anything about a vampire. But I sure as hell am gonna tell 'em about those girls!"

She started to say something, and he shrugged out of her grasp, then stormed around her and threw open the door. "Charley!..." she began, but he refused to acknowledge her.

The door slammed shut behind him.

Leaving Amy sick with fear of something nameless. The term "paranoid psychotic" was not an active part of her vocabulary.

"You're sure about this, now." It was not so much a question as a pronouncement, with the unspoken context *if you're lying, I will screw you into the wall.*

The voice in question was deep and booming. It emanated from the massive form of Lieutenant Detective Lennox. He was a homicide cop from the Rancho Corvallis force, and he wasn't used to being busy. He also wasn't used to having his ass on the griddle: screaming from the populace, pressure from on high. And there had been a lot of cranks calling in on the case, a lot of wild geese that he'd grown tired of chasing.

Lennox was one of the few black men on the Rancho Corvallis force; he was also the first. He had a short gray Afro that was rapidly turning white and a mustache that was black against his dark chocolate complexion. He wore a severe gray suit, gray vest, white shirt, striped tie pulled tight. He had no neck. He looked eminently capable of screwing Charley into a wall.

It was not a pleasant thought for Charley. He nodded emphatically at the cop, prayed to God that he *hadn't* been imagining things, and then the two of them started up the walk to the Dandrige house.

Someone watched them from behind the curtains. Charley could see the shadowed silhouette in the window. It sent a shiver of dread through him that refused to go away, getting worse with every step he took.

They reached the door, and Lennox knocked firmly with his slab of a hand. The sound echoed through the silent house, an effect distinctly audible from the outside. It was as if they'd knocked on the door of a cave.

Footsteps followed, heavy and slow. Charley felt his fear grow nearly intolerable, prickling against the inside of his flesh.

The door opened.

It was the man who had caught him at the storm doors. He didn't look any prettier than he had the day before. Even when he smiled, as he was doing right now, there was something cold and unpleasant about him. *Something foul*, Charley thought, and an image of maggots crawling through raw meat came unbidden.

"Yes?" the man said, looking from Lennox to Charley and back again.

"Mr. Dandrige?" the detective said.

"No. I'm Billy Cole, his roommate. Why?"

"Lieutenant Lennox. Homicide." He flashed his badge. Billy's eyes widened in what looked like genuine surprise. "Mind if we come in?"

"Not at all." Billy stepped aside, allowing them entrance. Lennox entered first, automatically pocketing the badge. Charley followed, forcing himself to make eye contact, forcing down his fear. The face of his host was inscrutable.

Then he began to look around.

The foyer was huge, with black and white checkerboard tiles in the floor, each tile roughly two feet square. Two black, foreboding statues framed the foot of a massive, Gothic-looking staircase. The place was as imposing as the inside of a cathedral, though somewhat more sinister in tone.

The effect was mitigated slightly by the cardboard boxes stacked in the area, most of them not yet unpacked. There were also several pieces of heavy Victorian furniture, some of them covered with white dropcloths. They did *not* diminish the effect.

Charley checked out some of the stuff in the boxes, making his investigation casual. Nothing out of the ordinary showed: towels, clothes, unexceptional knick-knacks and household goods. He wondered if vampires took showers and stuff. He wondered if they needed to brush their teeth, or woke up in the middle of the day because they needed to take a leak.

Reaching no conclusions, he followed Billy and Detective Lennox into the living room, which was also full of unpacked boxes and crates. As they left the foyer, however, Charley noticed that one wall was completely lined with clocks.

None of them working.

All of them set for six o'clock.

"Is there anything I can help you with?" Billy asked when they had stopped walking.

"There've been a couple of murders," Lennox replied. He was, at this point, taking Charley seriously enough to keep his eye on Cole at all times. "This young man lives next door, and he claims to have seen two of the victims at your house in the last few days."

Cole looked shocked. "Oh, you're kidding!" Lennox shook his head. Charley looked for a chink in Billy's façade, didn't find one. "This is ridiculous. Nobody's come to visit since we got here. No Welcome Wagons, no nothing." He grinned.

"That's a lie," Charley blurted. The two men turned to him appraisingly. He felt himself blush as he continued. "I saw him carry a body out in a plastic bag last night."

Billy laughed. It didn't sound phony. "That's terrific," he said. "I know exactly what he saw. Where he got this *body* business is something else again, but..." He shrugged disarmingly and took a couple of steps into the debris.

"Here," he concluded, stooping to pick up a large Hefty bag. It was stuffed with wrapping paper and mashed cardboard boxes. He brandished it like a trophy.

"The bag I saw had a body in it," Charley insisted, low.

"Did you actually see a body?" Skepticism was beginning to reemerge on Lennox's face.

"Well... *no*, but..."

"But what?"

"... but I saw two girls here; one of 'em coming in, the other one through the window. They were the two girls on the news, I swear to God." The words came out in a flurry. He was afraid that he wouldn't get to finish.

"That's completely ridiculous," Billy insisted. He looked pissed now, and Charley had no doubt that it was genuine. "I think our young friend is lying through his teeth," he continued, turning to Lennox. "That's completely off the wall. Look, how about if I take you around back and show you what's in all of our garbage bags?"

"He didn't take the bag I'm talking about out back," Charley insisted. "He put it in the Jeep and drove it away."

Billy made a disgusted, impatient face. Lennox's sympathy with Cole was obvious.

"Look. I can prove he's lying," Charley said. "Let's look in the basement instead."

"What's in the basement, Charley?" Detective Lennox asked.

"Yes," Billy echoed, turning to lock his eyes with Charley. "What's supposed to be in the basement, Charley?"

Charley couldn't move. He couldn't speak. There was something in Billy's eyes that held him. Not hypnosis, not supernatural mind control, not anything heavier than basic mortal dread. Charley saw the menace that lurked behind the eyes, saw it clearly. He wished that Lennox would see it, too.

But Lennox didn't see. Lennox was getting impatient. Seconds ticked past with ruthless precision, and still Charley couldn't speak. And still Billy bored into him with his eyes. And still Lennox waited, tapping his foot now, waiting for the moment to break.

It did, at last, Billy turning to the detective and saying, "I think it's pretty clear that the kid doesn't know what he's talking about." He was about to continue when something snapped inside Charley Brewster, forcing the words that he did not want to say out of his throat.

"It's a coffin!" he yelled. "That's what's down there: a coffin! I saw them carry it in!"

"*What?*" Lieutenant Detective Lennox looked like he'd been knocked for a loop.

"Yeah," Charley continued. "And you'll find Jerry Dandrige in it, sleeping the sleep of the undead!"

"What are you *talking* about?" Lennox was utterly mystified now.

"He's a *vampire!*" Charley practically screamed. "I saw him last night, through the upstairs bedroom window! He had fangs, and I watched him bite into her neck!"

"Oh, for Christ's sake," the detective muttered. He grimaced, the full weight of human stupidity pressing down on the corners of his mouth. Then he grabbed Charley roughly by the arm and said, "C'mon. We're going outside."

"But..."

"No *buts.*" Lennox didn't shout, but he might as well have. Charley could feel his head being drilled into the wall already.

They moved toward the front door: Lennox pulling, Charley dragging along, Billy following languidly behind. The cop wasn't looking at Billy Cole's face, but Charley was. It was not the face of an innocent man. He leered as they reached the door, which Lennox threw open. Then it softened as the detective turned and said, "I'm sorry, Mr. Cole."

"Anytime." Billy was smiling.

Lennox virtually tossed Charley through the doorway and onto the porch, then followed after. Cole shut the door behind them. Lennox quickly grabbed Charley's arm again and dragged him down the walkway to his car.

"I oughtta take you in," the cop hissed. "I oughtta take you in on a goddam charge of obstructing justice and nail your little ass to the floor. I could do that, you know? I could do that with ease."

"I wasn't lying," Charley insisted. He was scared and hurt and angry enough to piss himself and slug Lennox simultaneously. "Jerry Dandrige *is* a vampire! If you just woulda *looked—*"

"Now listen, kid." Lennox slammed Charley into the side of the police cruiser—not hard enough to damage, but enough to show that there was more where that came from. "And listen good. If I ever see you down at the station house again, I'm gonna throw you in jail. And I don't mean overnight."

"But..."

Lennox wasn't listening. He pushed Charley aside, threw open the car door and slid inside. The door slammed shut.

"*Please*, sir! I'm—"

The cruiser's engine kicked in with a murderous roar.

"—I'm telling the *truth!* I'm—"

Rubber and asphalt came together in a squeal of motion. The car fired away from the curb like a bottle rocket, tearing down the street.

"THEY'RE GONNA KILL ME!" Charley screamed, and then Lennox and his vehicle screeched around the corner, disappearing from view forever.

The front door of the Dandrige house creaked open. Billy Cole stood there.

He was smiling.

Eight

The door went flying inward and Charley followed suit. There was a narrow flight of stairs directly before him. He took them two at a time.

"EDDIE!" he hollered. "EDDIE!"

Evil Ed's room was at the end of the hall. Charley sprinted toward it, not thinking about the members of the Thompson household, not thinking about anything but the coppery taste of horror on his tongue. When he reached Ed's door, he threw it open.

Evil Ed was parked in front of his desk. He held a delicate paintbrush in his right hand and a hideous monster model in his left. It was The Ghoul, as advertised in the back pages of *Famous Monsters of Filmland*. Like the magazine, it was old, and had been out of distribution for many years. Ed had the whole set, treasured them enormously and periodically did touch-up work on their bloody jaws and pasty green complexions.

He was doing so now, and he didn't appear thrilled at the interruption. "And to what," he said, cocking one eyebrow disdainfully, "do I owe this dubious pleasure?"

"You gotta help me!" Charley gasped, out of breath.

Eddie sneered. "That's Amy's department."

"No, no! You don't understand! The vampire knows that I know about him."

"What?"

51

"The vampire! He knows... or he will when he wakes up. Shit!" Charley glanced at his watch. It was four thirty-five.

Eddie glanced at his own watch instinctively, then looked back at Charley, disgusted. "What vampire are you referring to? There are so *many* of them, you know."

He gestured snidely around the room. It was a virtual monster museum. Posters of old Karloff/Lugosi/Chaney, Jr. screamfests covered the walls. The rest of his models shared bookshelf space with half a ton of paperback horror novels, a boxed set of vintage *Tales From the Crypt*, complete collections of *Creepy*, *Eerie* and *Vampirella* and a vast assortment of creepy rubber monstrosities.

Charley stamped his foot, gritted his teeth and tried to pull himself together. "Look, I'm not kidding. A vampire moved into the house next door, and it's going to kill me if I don't protect myself."

"Right." Eddie snorted. "You're a fruitcake, Brewster, I swear to God."

"You've got to believe me!"

"No, I don't."

"But—"

"Listen." Evil Ed gestured impatiently with his paintbrush. "I don't know what *your* problem is, but it isn't mine. Understand? Ever since you started hanging out with Amy, I've hardly seen you. You never have time, you never have anything nice to say. It seems to me like you sorta wrote me off. So I'm writing *you* off. Hit the road."

"Eddie, please." Charley's voice had gotten softer. The truth of his old friend's words—his ex-friend, from the sound of it—hit home. "I'm sorry. You're right. But I really need your help. I'm scared."

"You've got a vampire living next door." Evil Ed nodded his head condescendingly. "Okay. I can see why you're scared. Fer sure." He grinned at The Ghoul and said, dotingly, "You'd be scared, *too*, wouldn't you, Punkin'?"

52

"Don't make fun of me!" The outburst of anger seemed sudden, but it had been building for a while. "I'm getting tired of everybody treating me like I'm crazy!"

"Yeah, *tell* me about being treated like you're crazy!" Ed roared back. *"Tell* me about everybody treating you like an asshole! You don't think I know what that's like? You don't think people treat me like that every day of my life?

"Well, think again, Brewster! and then think about dragging your tail out the door! You can't treat me like shit for three months and then just barge in here, demanding that I drop everything and run off to hunt a stupid fucking vampire with you!"

Tense silence. The two boys stared at each other. Evil Ed Thompson, surprised by his own fury, took a deep breath before continuing in a level, weary voice.

"You got a vampire, Charley? Go hunt it yourself. You know what to do, right? Unless you've forgotten *everything* about the last four years."

Charley mutely shook his head.

"Fantastic. If you kill it, I'd be thrilled to check out the moldering bones. If it kills you... well, I guess I'll just have to keep my wood stakes handy, right?"

Silence.

"You'd *like* to put a stake through my heart, wouldn't you?" Charley said softly. "It would make you feel better, right?"

"Don't flatter yourself." Evil Ed turned back to his desk, dipped his paintbrush in the murky green liquid, started dabbing at The Ghoul's face again. "Get lost."

Charley didn't bother to close the door behind him.

Nine

All the way home, Charley couldn't stop thinking about what Evil Ed had said. It hurt on so many levels, in so many different ways. *You know what to do, right?* was the phrase that kept ringing in his ears. Followed by *unless you've forgotten* everything *about the last four years...*

"Four years," he said aloud to the empty car. It was funny to count down the days like that, look back over a quarter of his total lifespan and think, *Yeah, Eddie and I have been best friends since seventh grade. We used to hang out constantly: playing crazy games, reading comics, watching* Fright Night *together...*

His mental processes stopped with that name. *Fright Night.* It conjured up images of a million vampire sieges, in glorious color or somber black and white. It conjured up pictures of Peter Vincent, standing tall against the undead hordes that slavered for the blood of the innocent.

It conjured up scenes of bloody horror, substituting Charley himself for every bloodless victim ever flashed across the screen.

And it conjured up a battle plan: his only hope of salvation.

Charley veered left on Rathbone Avenue, whipped sharply into the parking lot of the Super-Saver shopping center. The Mustang screeched into the first available space and died promptly at a twisting of the key. He threw open the door, not bothering to lock it, and slammed it shut as he ran toward the complex of stores.

He hoped that they had what he needed.

Darkness had already fallen when the last nail was slammed home. The darkness hung outside the window, chill and bloated as the corpse of a drowned man. Charley stared out into it for a moment, then stepped back to appraise his handiwork.

The window had been secured with ten-penny nails he'd acquired from Carradine Hardware. Garlic from the Super-Saver was strung around it in garlands, using thread from Reisinger's. There hadn't been any holy water, but plastic crucifixes were cheap and plentiful; he'd picked up three, kept one constantly at his side. The hammer and the needle were household property; he'd put them back in a minute, once he was satisfied with the job.

Other pieces of vampire lore were floating around in his mind. He hadn't gotten around to whittling stakes yet, though there were some good slats of grape fence out in the garage that made prime candidates. No *way* was he going out of the house until morning. That was certain. If Jerry Dandrige wanted him, Jerry Dandrige would have to come and get him.

That was the other thing that made him feel reasonably secure. If everything he'd ever seen about vampires held true, they couldn't come into your house without being invited. He knew that *he* sure as hell wouldn't be sending out invitations.

His mother's voice cut through the clamor of his thoughts. "Charley?" it called. "Come down here for a moment, would you, please?"

"Just a second, Mom!" he called back, feigning cheerfulness. "I just gotta finish something!"

Quickly he pushed a heavy chest of drawers in front of the window. It probably wouldn't help, if worse came to worst, but it sure didn't hurt.

Then he trotted down the hall, hit the stairs and rapidly descended. The physical work had invigorated him, made him feel more confident. He was almost in a good mood when he entered the living room and said "What?"

His mother was standing in the living room, a drink in her hand. She was beaming.

"Honey?" she said. "There's somebody I'd like you to meet."

That was when he glanced at the old quilted chair. His father's chair, high-backed and nearly heart-shaped, which only special guests had used in the seven years since...

There was somebody sitting in the chair. Charley couldn't see his face, hidden by the chairback's curving wings. But the hand that protruded from the man's tweed jacket was long-fingered, almost feminine. There was an expensive diamond ring glimmering brightly on one pale-white finger.

Charley's breath caught in his throat. *This can't be happening.*

His mother's guest leaned forward, smiled and skewered him with its eyes.

"Hi, Charley," the vampire said. "I've heard so much about you."

Charley's jaw dangled slackly. If all the saliva in his mouth hadn't dried up in terror, he might have drooled. All the muscles in his body were jammed. He couldn't move. He couldn't breathe. He could only stare at the monster before him with moist and bulging eyes.

Jerry Dandrige was beautiful. There was no way around it. Jerry Dandrige was quite possibly the best-looking man that Rancho Corvallis had ever seen. His smile was impish, and infinitely amused. His dark eyes sparkled with intimate knowledge. Up close, his charisma was overwhelming. Charley could see why the girl in the window had danced with him.

Now the vampire was doing the same thing to his mother.

Judy Brewster looked like a teenage girl on the Beatles' first American tour; all she needed was a mob around her to start screaming and crying and tearing at Dandrige's clothes. As it was, her basic perkiness had accelerated to fever pitch. She was falling all over herself, giggling and fawning and oozing desire.

It was disgusting. Worse yet, it was terrifying. Charley had a nightmare feeling that Jerry could drain his blood right there and Mom would ask him if he wanted another drink. *And she'd giggle while she said it*, he added sickly.

Jerry Dandrige stood. He was only a little bit taller than Charley, but he might as well have been Goliath. "I've been looking forward to this," he said, moving closer.

Charley still couldn't move, but he was dangerously close to soiling his underwear. *Omigod*, his mind silently intoned, *I'm gonna die, I'm gonna die...*

... as the vampire closed to within a foot of him.

Stopped.

And extended a hand in greeting.

"Well, say *'hello'* to Mr. Dandrige, honey!" his mother piped. She turned, as if confidentially, to Jerry and added, "I don't know what's *wrong* with him sometimes! Honest to goodness, we didn't raise him like that!"

(Say "hello," Charley.)

"Hi," Charley said. He had no choice in the matter. Nor could he stop his right hand from coming up and engaging with Dandrige's in what looked like a hearty handshake.

(That's right.)

The vampire was controlling him. Charley's mind was fully conscious of the fact; but his will was gone, his bodily motion out of his hands.

(Fun, isn't it? Now let go.)

The handshake ended. The connection did not. Jerry Dandrige had him; his ears and mind picked up two different conversations at once.

"Your mother was kind enough to invite me over," the vampire said. His voice was thick with honeyed sexuality, sweet and musky all at once. "I might never have made it over here

(But you knew that, didn't you?)

58

otherwise. But now she tells me that I'm welcome any old time. Like

(In the middle of the night...)

tomorrow, for lunch... which, unfortunately, I won't be able to make. But I told her that I'll be having friends over in the weeks to come, and she offered to bring the refreshments

(Like everybody she knows...)

over. Isn't that great?"

(Say "yes.")

"You bet!" Charley enthused with an emotion that was not his own. He could feel his lips twisting themselves into a smile. It was like being force-fed slime, but he couldn't even crinkle his nose with disgust.

Then Mom stepped between them, starry-eyed and beaming. "It's so m*arvelous* that you're getting along so well!" she crowed.

And the connection was broken...

... and Charley staggered backward, mewling faintly, his flesh gone so white that he looked like he'd been bitten. His mother stared after him, stunned, as he hit an end table and sent it clattering to the floor. The vampire just smiled and smiled.

"CHARLES ALAN BREWSTER!" his mom shouted imperiously. "What on earth is *wrong* with you?"

Keep it together, Charley's mind informed him. *He'll kill us both right now if I don't keep it together.* He stopped, stooped and righted the table with jittering hands. "Sorry, Mom," he chirped in a falsetto of terror. "I just gotta get back to my homework, that's all."

"Well, be *careful!*" she advised cheerfully. "I wouldn't want anything to happen to my baby boy!"

"No," the vampire echoed, grinning. "We certainly wouldn't want *that!*"

Dandrige's good-bye was the last thing Charley saw before turning to race up the stairs.

And into the safety of his room.

He *hoped*.

Ten

The shadows.

Charley sat, mesmerized by the oblong fingers of blackness that curled around the window.

Shadows. No big deal. Same damn shadows that had been there for the last twelve years. Same tree, same streetlight, same simple gradations of light and dark.

So why are they making my flesh crawl? he thought.

He sat, as he'd been sitting for the past five hours, staring fixedly out his bedroom window. The cheap plastic crucifix was threatening to come apart in his hands, the gold leaf staining his fingers. He'd been rubbing it like a prize Labrador retriever for the better part of the evening.

Ever since the light came on.

Just as he'd begun to recover from Dandrige's visit, the vampire's bedroom light had blinked on. Charley ducked reflexively, his heart doing Tito Puente in his chest, and crouched there a good three minutes before daring to venture a peek.

The light was still on, but the shade was down. No discernible movement, no furtive displays. Nothing. It just sat there, throbbing like a beacon.

Or a lure.

Charley watched, and waited. For what, he was too frightened to think. His room, dark but for his flickering Coors sign, strobed incessantly. The light in the window of the Dandrige house pulsed, ever so slightly out of sync. The tree threw its long, black fingers across the yard, rustling softly in the night air.

Eventually, Charley slept.

In his dream, he flew. He soared through the night, high above Rancho Corvallis on leathery wings, the wind rushing past and filling his ears with whispers, many many voices that melded together to form one all-encompassing howl, a night cry, harsh and sweet.

He arched, tiny jaws yawning to reveal tiny sharp teeth, and screamed, a high, chittering song. He swooped and caught a moth, rolling in mid-flight, and crunched it in his mouth, savoring the juice.

Wanting more.

He rolled and dove back to earth, to the safe, staid little homes, their soft, sleeping occupants oblivious to the nightsong, and yearned to swoop down and bury sharp teeth in their soft, stupid throats.

Something hit the roof with a thud. Charley jerked upright in his chair, heart racing. He shook his head, trying to dispel the tatters of the dream.

"Huh wubba?" he mumbled, staring at the ceiling. He listened hard, heard only the familiar night sounds of the house he grew up in. The soft rush of air through the heating ducts. The bubbling of the aquarium. The hum of the no-frost refrigerator down in the kitchen, doing its duty. His mom, snoozing away.

The creak of beams in the attic.

The attic?! Charley jumped straight out of his chair. The creaking of the beam was soft but regular, moving away from him. Soft and regular...

Like footsteps.

Mustering all his bravado, Charley moved gingerly toward the door. He opened it a crack, poked his head out cautiously, ready to retreat at a moment's notice.

"Mom?" His voice came out a squeak. "Mom, are you out there?"

The hallway was empty, and deadly silent. He crept out, feet making little *whuffing* sounds on the shag carpeting. He tiptoed to his mother's door, opened it a crack.

Judy Brewster lay peacefully, mask in place, sleeping the sleep of the just. A bottle of Nytol was perched on the bedside table, within easy reach.

Something was downstairs now. A sound, faint yet palpable, emanating from the darkened portico. Like fingernails on glass.

Soft.

Relentless.

Charley's knees wobbled. With Mom tucked away, that greatly narrowed the possibilities of who was making that sound. He didn't want to think about that. Not in the dark, alone. He had to check it out, though.

Hey, no big deal, he thought, fooling no one. *S'probably mice or something. Sure...*

He gripped his crucifix a little tighter and went downstairs.

Charley stood in the portico, breathing a sigh of relief. The creepy scratching noise that reverberated through the entire living room had revealed itself to be a tree branch, scraping harmlessly against the window. Charley felt a flood of relief. *So much for things that go bump in the night,* he thought, and detoured through the kitchen for some munchies.

He didn't notice, as he made his way to the kitchen, that the scratching stopped.

Jerry Dandrige stood calmly gazing down at the sleeping form of Judy Brewster. He took the room in at a glance: the wonderfully cheesy furniture (*Nouveau moustique, très chic, madame!*), the boudoir scattered with wigs and cosmetics, the infamous Judy Brewster herself (*Well, hel-loooo! Come in! Can I get you a drink? Tee-heeee...*) deep in repose.

It was too easy.

He touched her briefly, contempt mingling with the longing for her hot blood. She smiled, a nocturnal fantasy in motion. Then he turned past the open window and glided across the floor.

He paused as he passed the boudoir mirror, smiled wickedly. "You know," he purred, "you look *marvelous!*"

No reflection smiled back.

When he shut the door behind him, he very nearly yanked it off its hinges.

Charley never heard his mother's door crack shut. He was immersed in constructing a sandwich, head buried in the fridge.

He put the last finishing touches on it, a certifiable Dagwood—bologna, salami, turkey roll, three kinds of cheese and pickles—and munched it noisily all the way up the stairs...

... scarcely glancing at his mother's door.

He padded down the hall softly, shouldering open his door. Took another big bite before sliding inside. Locked the door, pushing his desk chair under the knob. Sat down, turned on the TV, took another big bite...

... and felt the tiny hairs rise on the back of his neck.

He turned around very slowly, so as to give the bad feeling plenty of time to *go away*. No such luck. His sensory information registered in microseconds, each one progressively worse than the last, until he had turned quite far enough.

And he and the vampire were face to face.

Charley wanted to run. He wanted to scream. If a coordinated air strike could be arranged, he wanted one of those, too.

As it was, the best he could manage was to leap out of his chair, spraying bits of partially chewed sandwich through the air.

The vampire lashed out casually and caught Charley's throat in a vise-lock grip, shutting off his air supply without a squeak. He smiled magnanimously.

"Now, now... we wouldn't want to wake your dear mother, *would* we, Charley? That would be a *terrible* thing to do, wouldn't it?" The vampire nodded. Charley nodded. The vampire smiled. Perfect teeth. "Because then I'd have to kill her, too. Right?" He tightened his grip infinitesimally. The pain was excruciating.

Charley nodded. He had no choice. The vampire worked his head like a ventriloquist works his dummy. Up and down, up and down. *Yes, Boss, anything you say, Boss.*

"Right," the vampire concluded, flinging Charley the length of the room with such force that he smashed clear through the dry wall, leaving an enormous gaping hole. Charley slid down the wall and lay in a crumpled heap.

Dandrige sauntered across the floor as if on a fashion runway. Coolly elegant, reeking of menace. He picked Charley up one-handed—all 167 pounds of him— without even leaning to support the load. Charley's eyes swam in his head as if he were a steer in a slaughterhouse, his brain going *MAYDAY MAYDAY MAYDAY MAYDAY...*

"Do you realize the trouble you've caused me? Spying on me, almost disturbing my sleep this afternoon, telling *policemen*"—he tightened his grip—"about me?"

He slammed Charley into the wall for emphasis. Charley wondered dimly how many successive slams it would take to induce complete renal failure. His face was the color of ptomaine poisoning. Jerry leaned in.

"You deserve to die, boy, and I think you should. But then, that could be messy. Too close to home." The vampire smiled. "You see, I *like* my privacy. And I like this town. In fact, I'd like to stay here for a long, long time." He loosened his grip on Charley, but continued holding him pinned to the wall. Charley gasped for breath.

"Of course, I could give you something you saw fit to deny *me:* a choice. Shall we make a deal, hmmm? You forget about me, I forget about you. "Whaddaya say, Charley?"

Charley fumbled, his life in the balance.

Then he remembered his cross.

He wormed his hand into his pocket and started to whip it out. Dandrige caught his wrist on the way out and pulled it up and away, threatening to dislocate his shoulder in the process. Charley yelped, and got his head slammed into the wall for his trouble.

"Not so easy, Chuck. I have to *see* it." Jerry held his hand at arm's length and squeezed until Charley couldn't take it anymore. The crucifix dropped to the floor.

"If you k-k-kill me, everybody'll be s-suspicious," Charley blurted. "My m-mother, the police..."

The vampire paused a moment, then smiled beatifically.

"Not if it looks like an accident." He yanked Charley over to the window, pushing away the heavy dresser with one foot. "A fall, for instance." He flipped the lock, started pulling the nails out one by one with a dainty *he loves me, he loves me not* cadence. " 'Disturbed teenager with paranoid fantasies about *vampires*, of all things, suffers a nasty fall while trying to barricade his bedroom.' "

He swung Charley around, opening the window with a flourish. "'A terrible tragedy for all concerned, of course. But lately he had seemed so *withdrawn*, Officer, and you know what they say about suicidal teens...'"

Slowly, inexorably, Dandrige pushed back and back, easing Charley out the window. The boy kicked and clawed like a maniac, legs splaying wildly, arms thrashing, hands searching for any hold. His right hand found purchase on the windowsill, and he twisted his torso in the killing grip to find something more substantial.

Dandrige eased up momentarily before dealing the final push. After all, *any d*eath—even one as stupid and trivial as this—deserved to be savored.

Charley seized in desperation upon the lessened pressure. Bowing his back painfully, he lurched to the left, hand raking wildly across his desk.

The night yawned black beneath him, the cold earth a good thirty feet below.

The vampire resumed pushing. Its strength was overwhelming. "Tut tut, Charley. We don't want to keep Mother Night waiting."

Charley clawed the desk surface blindly, groping for anything.

And finding...

A pencil. His fingers curled around it. He started to slide.

Charley brought the pencil around in a blind arc that would have pierced his own throat had it missed. Instead it plowed home, impaling the dead flesh of the vampire's hand. Dandrige howled and jerked back, hissing like a cat.

Charley scrambled to regain his equilibrium. His back felt as if someone had tied him to a belt-sander. *Great*, his mind raced. *Now I'll fall out all by myself.* He pulled himself in, coughing and sputtering...

... as Dandrige began to change.

First came the odor of overwhelming decay, a ripe stench of death too long denied. It hit Charley like a wave, making his gorge rise and his ears fill with the buzzing of many flies. Barely able to stand it, helpless to turn away, Charley stood slack-jawed with lurid fascination as the horror unfolded before him.

His room had been transformed into a nightmare detail from a Hieronymus Bosch painting, a livid slice of Hell pinwheeling around amid the sports-car posters and ski paraphernalia, howling and cursing in a harsh, guttural tongue. The Coors sign winked like a malevolent red eye, casting a pale glow on the room.

Jerry Dandrige writhed and spit, too overtaken with pain and indignation to remain calm in the face of this affront. He held out his wounded hand, the pencil still protruding. A faint plume of acrid smoke wafted up from the puckered hole, mixed with the stench of charred wood.

The vampire halted suddenly, hunkering over. Charley's breath was ragged in his chest. His heart skipped a beat as the vampire whirled to face him.

Charley winced. His face was the worst.

Gone were the smooth, affluent good looks that had floored his mother. The real Jerry Dandrige was an ancient, misshapen creature with a jutting lower jaw that gaped open to reveal a host of foul yellow teeth. Its hair was coarse and brittle, its ears deformed and pointed flaps. The skin of its face was sallow and collected in hideous, liver-spotted pockets, gathering most noticeably ground its eyes.

Its eyes...

Sunken, red-rimmed pits. They burned, luminous and bulging, boring holes straight through Charley's skull. Sapping him. The muscles in his back went slack, and he fell against the crushed wall on shaking legs.

Unable to pull away.

The vampire hissed then, and grasped the pencil with long crooked fingers, its nails clicking together with a chitinous sound. It fixed Charley with a stark, imperious look that did little to conceal its agony.

And pulled the pencil out.

Charley grimaced. The tip was blackened and still smoking. It tossed the pencil away contemptuously, and he noted sickly that a shred of withered flesh still clung to the tip, fluttering like a banner as it fell to the floor.

The vampire smiled, a horrible withered rictus. It felt *much* better. The pain was receding, as was the shock of this boy's impudence. *They always were clever in desperation,* it noted.

Its appearance improved enormously as its anger subsided. Its features smoothed and tightened, its hair thickened, and some semblance of humanity returned.

But the eyes still glowed red. The nails still clicked. And the teeth...

Jerry Dandrige gazed at Charley intently. He held up his hand, the wound gaping. "See the trouble you caused me, boy?" he said, advancing for the kill.

Charley's bowels turned to water. "*Noooo...*" he whined helplessly.

And then his mother started screeching at the end of the hall.

"DAMN!" The vampire whirled, hissing sibilantly. *Should've killed her when I had the chance.*

He turned back to the boy, who was leaning against the wall like a sack of potatoes on stilts. He wanted to trash the kid right here and now, be done with it forever. But no, he'd wait. *Plenty of time*, he thought, fighting back the urge to rend and tear.

The past centuries had taught him nothing if not patience. He cast one last appraising glance at Charley and hissed again, quite involuntarily.

"CHAR-LEY!" Mrs. Brewster caterwauled from her end of the hall, the *rattlerattlerattle* of her hand on the doorknob persistent. "SOMETHING'S WRONG WITH MY DOOR!"

Charley dimly perceived the vampire bolting from the room. He hadn't felt this high since he'd had his wisdom teeth out. His carotid arteries were working overtime to compensate for the constricted blood flow he'd experienced, courtesy of Dandrige's grip. It took a full ten seconds for the message to cut through the fog.

"MOM!" He stumbled out of his room, hoping he wasn't too late.

But his mom was okay. She stumbled out of her room, fumbling past the wreckage of her door. Charley cast about wildly, half expecting some kind of surprise attack.

The window at the end of the hall had been thrown wide open. Dandrige was gone, for now. Charley didn't know whether to breathe a sigh of relief or wet his drawers. He sighed, cold sweat sheening his back.

"Charley, what happened?"

Oh, nothing, Mom. I was just attacked by the vampire you were neighborly enough to have over for a drink, and he tried to kill me. That's all.

"I... I just had a nightmare, Mom. What happened to your door?"

Judy looked puzzled. "Why, I don't know!" She brightened. "But, you know, I had a nightmare just last night! I was at this white sale, and there I was, standing at the counter, and I reached for my credit cards, and suddenly I realized I was naked as the day I was born—"

She stopped abruptly as the sudden wrenching of metal and crunching of safety glass filled the night. It continued for several vicious seconds.

Then silence.

Judy just stared blankly at the open window at the end of the hall. The one that overlooked the back yard. And the garage.

"Now, what on earth was *that*?" She took a step toward the window, still woozy from her sleep aids. Charley grabbed her gently but firmly by the arm and wheeled her around.

"Nothing, Mom. Just the raccoons in the garbage again. No big deal. Why don't you just go back to sleep?"

Judy smiled. "But what about your nightmare, son? Do you want a nice Valium?"

Charley eased her through the door of her room. "I'm fine now, honest. Go back to bed, okay?"

Judy offered no resistance. She yawned. "Well, I *do* need my sleep. I start the night shift tomorrow, you know."

"Yes, Mom. I know. Good night."

She paused, placed her hand lovingly against his cheek.

"Charley, you're so *good*..."

"G'night, Mom." He pulled her door shut, its hinges creaking loudly.

Back in his room, Charley slumped back in his comfy chair. He was exhausted. The TV flickered in the darkness with its sound down low, mumbling in the corner like someone's idiot cousin. The remains of his sandwich stared at him wanly.

He couldn't think about food. He couldn't even think about the destruction of his room, and how he'd ever explain it.

All he could think about at that moment was the sound from his garage. He'd spent enough time restoring that car to recognize the sound of someone trashing it. *The bastard.*

He gazed up at the Shelby poster on the wall. *In Memorium...*

The bastard.

He gazed sullenly at the TV. *Fright Night* again. It was just what he needed. His hand reached over to flick off the set.

And the phone rang.

Charley's heart beat a quick one-two in his chest. He leaned over and grabbed the receiver quickly. Held it away from himself for a moment, as if it were a dead animal. And slowly, very slowly, brought it up to his ear.

He had a fair guess who it was.

"I know you're there, Charley. *I can see you.*"

Charley slowly turned to face the window. Sure enough, there stood Dandrige, blithely staring holes into him. His handyman was kneeling before him, rapturously bandaging his wounded hand.

Dandrige smiled grimly. "I just destroyed your car, Charley..."

No shit, you bastard!

"... but that's nothing compared to what I'm going to do to you tomorrow night."

The vampire hung up slowly, lackadaisically. And pulled down the shade.

Charley sat, numbly watching the darkened window, the phone still in his hand. He sat like that until the harsh *ditditdit* of the phone snapped him out of it. He got up, cradled the receiver, and slumped back

71

onto the bed. Impending doom flooded him. He turned and gazed blankly at the TV.

The horror film dissolved into a commercial offering absurdly expensive miniatures certain to be cherished for generations. He was not impressed. Half a dozen other hucksters paraded across the screen to no avail before the dripping *Fright Night* logo returned. Charley turned up the sound.

Peter Vincent, cloaked and bedraggled, was in rare form. He turned with a flourish, almost colliding with a rubber bat that twitched and flopped on a nylon filament. He brushed the bat away.

"Welcome back, horror fans. I hope you're enjoying tonight's feature, *I, A Vampire, Part Two*. It's one of my best." He glanced around ominously. "Did you know a lot of people *don't* believe in vampires?"

The bat's tether broke. It fell to the floor with a muffled plop. The crew broke up, their laughter leaking into Peter's lapel mike.

Peter Vincent drew himself up to his full height, glowering. "But *I* do. Because *I* know they exist. I have faced them in all their guises: man, woman, wolf, bat." Charley watched, intent.

"And I have always won. That's why they call me 'The Great Vampire Killer.'" Someone in the studio repressed a giggle. Peter flashed a killing glance. Dramatic pause.

"Now, watch me prove it in *I, A Vampire, Part Two (Two Two Two...)*"

His voice faded out with a ludicrous echo as a much younger Peter Vincent appeared on the screen, stake and mallet in hand. The camera panned back to reveal an endless vaulted corridor, deep in some drafty castle.

Charley sat up, eyes glued to the screen. "Get him, Peter. Get him," he whispered.

And in that instant, an idea was born.

72

Eleven

Channel 13 occupied a nondescript red brick building on Cameron Mitchell Drive, the kind of four-lane divided highway that can be found in every city west of the Hudson River. Fast-food restaurants, gas stations and shopping malls pockmarked the land; miles of prefab suburban sprawl, giving way at the last moment to the tiny cluster of streets and buildings that marked downtown proper of Rancho Corvallis.

Peter Vincent slipped quietly out the side door, a trench coat draped across his shoulders. He quickly descended the stairs, hoping to make it across the parking lot without incident. The day had probably been the most dismal day of his life. He walked stiffly, with a forced dignity that belied his true feelings.

The fools, he thought. *Those cretinous swine. How dare they*—

"Hey, Mr. Vincent."

Vincent froze. He turned, slowly and stately, to face his public: a solitary, rather haggard-looking teenager, advancing on him with an eagerness that bordered on hunger. He smiled politely, placing his hand casually on the door handle of a Mercedes sport coupe.

"Mr. Vincent, could I speak to you for a moment? It's *terribly* important."

Vincent sighed deeply, deftly whisking a fountain pen from his vest pocket. "Certainly... what would you like me to sign?"

"Pardon me?"

Vincent looked at the boy balefully. He repeated himself carefully, as one might to a retarded child. "*What* would you like me to sign? Where is your autograph book? I *am* rather busy, you know."

Charley shrugged sheepishly. "No, sir. I was curious about what you said last night on TV. You know, about believing in vampires and stuff."

Vincent regarded him warily. "What about it?"

"Were you *serious?*"

"Absolutely. Unfortunately," he added dryly, "none of your generation seems to share that conviction." His eyes flared.

Charley stared at him. "What do you mean?"

Peter Vincent could contain his fury no longer. "What I *mean* is that I have been *fired*. I have been fired because it would appear that no one wants to see vampire killers anymore. Or vampires, either, for that matter. Apparently, all they want are demented madmen running around in ski masks, hacking up nubile young virgins. Now, if you'll excuse me..."

Charley stood slack-jawed as Peter Vincent stepped huffily away from the Mercedes and made his way across the parking lot toward an ancient and decrepit Rambler. He fell in several paces behind the actor.

"Mr. Vincent, wait! *I* believe in vampires!"

"That's nice," Peter Vincent threw over his shoulder. "If only there had been more of you, perhaps my ratings would have been higher."

The Rambler loomed near. Charley was getting desperate. "In fact, I have one living next door. Would you... would you help me *kill* it?"

Peter Vincent winced, stopped dead in his tracks. He turned and stared coldly at the boy. "Come again?"

Charley stood his ground. "I said, would you help me to kill it?"

Peter Vincent turned red as a pulsing artery. His voice came out in clipped, shrill tones. "Oh, that's

74

rich! That's just grand! Who put you up to this, boy? Murray? Olson? The whole damned imbecilic crew? Kick a man when he's down, one last parting shot to wish me *bon voyage*." Charley just stared. "And what did they promise *you?* A few extra quarters for your insufferable video games?"

They had reached his car. Vincent fished for his keys, couldn't find them.

"The *murders*, Mr. Vincent! The ones in the papers! They're being committed by a vampire and he lives next door to me!"

Peter Vincent turned, growing weary. "Not funny, son," he sighed. "The joke's over, you've done your duty. Now toddle off and play Pac-Man or something."

Charley was on the verge of losing it. He grabbed Peter Vincent by the lapels, surprising the actor almost as much as himself. "MR. VINCENT, I'M NOT JOKING! I'M DEADLY SERIOUS!"

The actor's eyes bulged slightly in their sockets. *A nut case,* he thought. *Perfect. I'll be fired, harassed and murdered, all in the same morning.* He peeled Charley's fingers delicately from his lapels.

"I'm dreadfully sorry, but there's nothing I can do." Charley backed off somewhat, and Vincent hurried to unlock his door.

"But you just said you believed in vampires..."

"I lied. Now leave me alone."

Charley stopped, momentarily stunned by the terseness of the actor's reply. Vincent seized on the moment to jump in his car and lock the door. Charley became frantic as he started the engine, revving wildly.

"Please, you have to listen to me! The vampire tried to kill me last night and trashed my car when he didn't succeed!" Charley beat on the window like a maniac. Peter Vincent threw the car into reverse, started backing out.

"He'll be coming back for me and if I don't get help, he'll *kill me—*"

Peter Vincent wheeled the car in a wide arc, Charley still banging on the window.

"You've got to believe me!"

Vincent cast one final look at the boy, regarding him as one might a rabid animal. He gunned the engine, the car screeching out of the parking lot.

"MR. VINCENT!"

Charley stood and watched helplessly as his last hope drove away.

Twelve

The phone rang often at the Thompson house, but it was never for Evil Ed. The occasional crank call at midnight Friday from a bunch of drunken jocks, sure; equally rarely, the same jocks, threatening to run his ass up the flagpole if he didn't help them cheat on their tests.

Other than that, a Thompson phone call could mean any one of twenty things: bowling, bridge, canasta, golf, The Tiki Room, The Golden Bear, Nick's Steak House, Vinnie's Pizza Heaven, the legion post, St. Vincent's Bingo, the body shop, the beauty parlor, poker, pool, the Super Bowl, "The Guiding Light," the *National Enquirer* or the rising cost of Hamburger Helper.

None of which had anything to do with Ed. They were the staples that held together the lives of Lester and Margie Thompson, his parents. They were jolly, robust, on-the-go people with scarcely a thought in their heads. They couldn't understand their scrawny son's hermit-crab existence. They couldn't understand why he didn't go out and meet people, join the crowd, get some fun out of life.

They couldn't understand that he really didn't like people very much. It was a concept that was utterly beyond them.

But they were stuck with each other, whether any of them liked it or not. A numb sort of truce had been arrived at, and life went on: Les and Marge in the social whirl, Eddie in his room.

When the phone rang, nobody guessed that it was for him.

Nobody would *ever* have guessed that it was a girl.

But it was, and ol' Marge was in a regular dither about it. "Oh, Eddie!" she squealed, leading him toward the Pepto-Bismol-pink wall phone in the kitchen. "What have you been *doing* that we don't know about?"

"I put an ad in the paper for sacrificial virgins," he quipped. She didn't laugh. She probably didn't even know it was a joke. Eddie groaned and let her drag him into the kitchen. One would have thought that he were being led down Death Row.

Still, there was a part of him that burned with curiosity. Who could possibly be calling, and what could they possibly want? He ran down the list of girls who had ever given him an appraising glance, so far as he knew: Gail Blumstein, Peggy Lint, Anita Hogg, Beryl O'Flynn. Oily-haired nose-pickers, every one of them. He hoped to God that none of them had worked up the nerve to call.

That left only one other possibility: a prank. The message of Brian dePalma's *Carrie* hadn't been lost on him: if they could find a way to fuck you up, they would. That was the sentence that God and the world had passed on misfits: *trap them and kill them.*

He knew his lot. He just wasn't very happy about it. So he was greatly apprehensive when he picked up the receiver and brought it to the side of his head. Like Russian roulette.

"Hello?" he said, trying to be strong.

"Hello, Eddie?" came from the other end. Pretty, soft, intensely feminine. Definitely not one of the dogs.

"Uh... yeah." His mind was boggling, his heart going pitter-patter. *Who is this?* he wondered, then echoed the question out loud.

"This is Amy Peterson. Charley's... friend." She sounded nervous and embarrassed and deeply worried. It took Evil Ed a moment to pick up on; he was too busy being disappointed and pissed. "I need to talk with you about something."

"What?" Snippy.

"Well..." and now her unhappy hesitation showed through clearly, "... have you noticed anything funny about Charley lately?"

"Other than his face, you mean?"

"I'm not kidding, Eddie. This is serious. He's acting really crazy, and it scares me."

"Yeah?" For some reason, it hadn't occurred to Evil Ed that Charley might have been losing it with everyone. "Yeah?" he repeated, running yesterday's conversation through his mind. He started to smile.

"Well, he did come over yesterday," he continued. "It was pretty demented. He said he needed my help, because—"

"Oh, God."

"—a vampire was trying to kill him. Is that the same story you got?"

"Yes. Oh, God." In his mind's eye, he could see her pacing and chewing on her knuckles. The image amused him.

"Sounds to me like your boyfriend has blown a gasket, kiddo. You might just want to gift-wrap him for Three Northeast."

"What?"

"The mental ward at Hammer Memorial Hospital."

"*Eddie!*" she cried, and her voice was so plaintive that it made him question his own warped sense of humor. "Please, stop making fun and talk with me for a minute. We've got to figure out what we're going to do—"

"Wait a minute," he cut in, not joking now. "Waitaminutewaitaminutewaitaminute. Hold your horses. Where do you get this 'we' business?"

"Well, I..." He'd yanked the rug out from under her on that one. It didn't feel as good as he'd thought it would. "I just thought that you'd want to help him," she rushed on. "You're his best friend, and—"

"I think we're speaking past tense, Amy. He *was* my best friend. Now he's just another jerk who ignores me in the halls. And if he wants to cut out paper dollies of Dracula, he can go right ahead. Just make sure that he uses safety scissors."

"That's really mean, Eddie."

"I'm *feeling* really mean, Amy. Not that anyone gives a shit. It seems to me that you all wouldn't be running to *my* assistance—"

"Yeah?" Now *she* sounded angry, and Evil Ed heard the distant sound of tables being turned. "What about the time when Chuck Powell and Butch Masey cornered you behind the cafeteria? Or that time in the woods out back of the football field?"

"How'd you know about that?" Evil Ed was on the defensive. The memory of that scene in the woods loomed up, pathologically vivid, in his mind's eye. He still had a scar on his right arm from the broken-off tree branch, its jagged edge raking a five-inch furrow across his bicep, Chuck and Butch and three other guys dragging him off the trail and throwing him down.

And who saved my ass? Evil Ed remembered sickly. *Who gave Chuck a black eye and knocked the wind out of Joey Boyle? Who?*

But the point was already made.

"Charley told me," she was saying. "Charley talks about you a lot. We'll be watching a movie on *Fright Night*, and he'll say, 'Evil Ed and I must've seen this one a dozen times.' Or we'll be sitting at Wally's, and he'll start talking about the time that you had all ten of the highest scores in Space Invaders—"

"That was a long time ago," he interrupted.

"Okay. Fine," she countered. "You're right. It's all ancient history. You are not your brother's keeper. God didn't make the little green apples, and—"

"*All right*, already!" he burst in angrily.

There was a taut moment of static and silence that stretched across the telephone wire.

"So what are we going to do?" he concluded.

"Mrs. Brewster?" Amy pushed open the kitchen door a little more, poked her head inside. "Mrs. Brewster? Charley? Anybody home?"

No answer. Just the mellow hum of the refrigerator. Amy turned to Evil Ed. They shrugged at each other and stepped inside.

At the foot of the stairs they heard the faint clacking of wood against wood. Then silence again. "Come on," Amy said, and they headed upstairs.

Charley's door was closed. A wafer-thin wedge of light poked out from underneath it, along with a delicate scraping sound. They paused for a moment, exchanged quizzical glances.

"What's he doing in there!" Eddie whispered in her ear.

"I don't know. But I think that we'd better find out."

"Let's do it."

They didn't notice the crucifix until they were nearly upon it. It was large and weighty, silver mounted on a thick mahogany base. It hung a foot above the "NO TRESPASSING" sign on his door, reflecting light.

They shared one last apprehensive glance. Then Eddie sighed, put his hand on the doorknob and twisted.

The full force of the room's transformation assailed them.

"Jesus Christ!" Eddie yelled. Charley's head jerked toward them suddenly; he yelped and jumped a foot out of his chair. Amy let out a little screech and brought her fists up to her mouth, eyes bulging with shock. The three of them stared at each other for a long silent moment.

"Jesus Christ," Evil Ed repeated quietly.

Charley's room had become a combination fortress/cathedral. Every square inch of table or desk space was covered with glowing candles. Dime-store crosses hung everywhere, vying for wallspace with the BMW and Mustang posters, overwhelming them at every turn. Huge strings of garlic were draped all around the window and over the bed.

On the floor at Charley's feet, a pair of rough-hewn wooden stakes lay one atop the other. They were carved from slats of grape fence: three feet long, five inches wide, three quarters of an inch thick. Charley had whittled them down to crude, ugly points.

A third one was in progress. He held the malformed embryo of it in his left hand, his old Boy Scout knife in his right.

Driven through a man's chest, any one of them would have taken a large portion of the heart with it, straight out the back and into the coffin's plush upholstery—given that the man was a vampire, at rest in his casket, a good daylight's distance from the cold dominion of the moon.

"You're probably wondering what I'm doing," Charley said.

"You got that right," Evil Ed replied. Amy, for the moment, was speechless.

"I'm getting ready," he said. "Dandrige can't get me if I stay in my room. The first time his little playmate leaves, I'm going over there and putting one of these things"—brandishing the stake in his hand—"through his goddam heart."

"But—" Amy started to say. It was the first sound she'd uttered since her opening screech.

"No," Charley stated. His voice was flat and blunt. "I don't want to hear about how I'm acting crazy. I don't want to hear about how I'm living in a fantasy world. I have a new next-door neighbor. He's a vampire. Last night, he almost killed me. I don't give a fuck whether *you* believe me, my *mother* believes me, *Peter Vincent* believes me, or not.

"There's an honest-to-God vampire next door, and he wants me to die because I know what he is. If you don't believe me, go to hell. I don't want to argue with you. I don't have time."

He went back to whittling his stake.

"Wait a minute," Evil Ed said finally. "What do you mean, 'whether Peter Vincent believes me or not'? Did you actually *talk* to him?"

"Yeah," said Charley, not looking up. A short, thin, curling slice of wood dropped to the floor like an autumn leaf.

"And what did he say?"

Charley spat out a bitter little chuckle. "Same as everybody else. I'm nuts." His blade stroked violently along the wooden shaft. "It doesn't matter."

"What do you mean, it doesn't matter? That's a pretty arrogant statement, if you don't mind my saying so. Has it ever occurred to you that you might be *wrong!*"

"Has it ever occurred to *you* that I might be *right!*" Charley stood up, quivering, stake and knife still in hand. "Dammit, did *that* ever occur to you? You didn't see him bite that girl in the neck! You didn't see him turn from a bat into a man! You didn't see him come in here and try to *kill* me last night!

"You don't know what the hell you're talking about!"

"Charley. *Please.*" Amy pleaded. It was almost a whisper. She was almost in tears. "This is crazy. You've got to stop—"

"Amy." Cold-faced, stern. "Do me a favor. Go home."

"We're only trying to help!" she blurted.

"Great. If you want to help, grab one of those stakes and come with me; it's the only kind of help I need. Otherwise, just go home, okay?"

"Amy, let's go," Evil Ed said quietly.

"But..." She whipped around to face him. Her eyes were moist and pleading for mercy.

"Come on. There's no point. He isn't going to listen to us." Evil Ed looked slightly disgusted with the whole thing.

"He's right," Charley concluded. "I'm not going to listen."

Amy and Charley stared at each other for a minute that dragged. Charley's expression was fixed with determination. Amy struggled for the same effect, but kept threatening to break down in tears.

"Come on," Evil Ed insisted. "Amy, let's go."

Amy nodded ever so slightly, her gaze dropping from Charley's. Slowly, she turned and headed for the door. Evil Ed smiled and stepped aside, motioning toward the hall. She stepped into the middle of the doorway, stopped, turned to face back into the room.

"I love you, Charley," she said.

Then she turned back, not waiting for a reaction, and left the room.

"Way to go, Brewster. You're a class act, all the way." Evil Ed leered, a bit wearily, and then followed her. "*Now* what do we do?" Amy wanted to know. They'd made it all the way out of the house in silence; now they were on the sidewalk out front, staring up at the flickering light behind Charley's shuttered window.

"This is pretty crazy," Evil Ed admitted. "I never thought Chucko would go this far off the deep end. I mean, did you look at those *stakes*?" Amy nodded grimly. "Can you imagine pounding one of those suckers through somebody's chest? It's like—"

"*Eddie!*" Her eyes were red and bulging. They looked scarier than any undead peepers Evil Ed had ever seen.

"Okay, okay. I'm sorry." He took a deep, indignant breath that showed just how sorry he really was. "And I do have a plan of sorts, though I don't know if it'll work."

"Really?" The menace in her eyes softened, turned to piercing concentration. "What is it?"

"Let's see..." Scratching his head exaggeratedly. "Do you have any money, for starters?"

"WHAT?" She was instantly furious. "YOU—"

"It's not for *me*, Amy! Jesus! Wouldja *relax* a second?"

84

She took a deeper, more indignant breath that showed just how relaxed she was really getting. Then she settled down to listen.

Two minutes later, she was starting to grin.

Three minutes later, she said, "I've got the money. No problem."

Four minutes later, they had cinched their roles in the horror to come.

Thirteen

It makes sense, mused Peter Vincent, *in the most perverse sort of way. The Fearless Vampire Killer falls prey, in the end, to the most terrifying bloodsuckers of them all.*

He held a handful of bills, all long overdue, many marked "last notice." One was an eviction notice, in fact, giving him three days to vacate his apartment. It was just the sort of cheeriness he required to make his single worst day in history complete.

"Damn it all," he announced to the room. The walls, and the endless memorabilia hanging from them, had no response. Evidently, over thirty starring roles in classics like *Blood Castle, Fangs of Night* and *I Rip Your Jugular* didn't mean anything. Nor did five years as the only ghost host in American late-night TV who could show his own films. Nor did those same five years spent in the same apartment under the pretense that the rest of his life was taken care of.

Peter Vincent was scared. More than that, Herbert McHoolihee was scared. The man behind the pseudonym had been cowering since he first auditioned for a bit part in *Fingers of Fear*. He'd gotten a bigger part than he'd bargained for, and Peter Vincent had been born. Twenty years of relative success at the top of his field had submerged the insecurities of little Herbert.

But as the heroic mask eroded, he came more and more to resemble poor Dorian Gray's portrait. His so-serious image had become ridiculous, even to his own eyes. His once-commanding features held no conviction. The weightiness of his former preeminence had become a 150-pound cinder block, attached to his neck by a stout length of chain and then lobbed into the river.

Herbert McHoolihee was drowning, and Peter Vincent couldn't save him. Now, at last, the dream was over.

And the nightmare was free to begin.

There was a knock on the door. The landlord, no doubt, come to verify receipt of the killing document. Peter moved wearily across the room and let the door creak open.

There were a couple of teenage kids in the doorway. The boy was a bit on the freaky side; he had electroshock-therapy hair and a manic, slightly crazed expression on his face. The girl was much straighter, with short brown curls and wide green eyes gracing a virginal, prom-queen appearance.

"Mr. Vincent," the girl said timidly. "May I speak with you for a moment?"

Peter got over his momentary surprise, assessed them briefly. They were clearly in earnest about something or other. Then he thought about the bills, and his empathy departed. "I'm afraid this isn't the best time—" he began.

"Please," the girl said, and there was no missing the desperation in her eyes, her voice. "It's terribly important."

"Ah, well," he sighed. "Come on in." A couple of minutes wouldn't hurt, he supposed. Perhaps give the old ego a bit of a boost. He bade them enter with a sweeping gesture, closed the door behind, and led them into the heart of the living room.

"Now what can I do for you?" he continued. "An interview for your school paper? Some autographs, perhaps?"

"No," the girl insisted. "I'm afraid this is much more important."

"Oh, really?" Frowning slightly.

"I know you're a very busy man, Mr. Vincent, but we're trying to save a boy's life."

"Well, yes." Harrumphing. "I can see where that might be more important."

"Would you care to explain yourself?"

"You remember a fruitcake named Charley Brewster?" the boy cut in. He had been gawking at the movie posters, with open admiration; now he stepped forward, focusing on the conversation. "He said he came to see you."

"No," Peter answered, wrinkling his brow with mock concentration as he shook his head.

"He's the one who thinks a vampire is living next door," the girl interjected.

"Ah, yes." Peter grinned as he spoke. "He's quite insane." Then he flashed a look of fatherly concern and said, "Dear me, I hope he's not a friend of yours."

"She's got the hots for him," the boy said, leering maliciously. The girl blushed and smacked him in the arm with her fist. He yelped.

"We need your help to stop him, Mr. Vincent. You see, he really does believe that his next-door neighbor is a vampire. He's planning to kill him."

"With a stake through the heart," the boy added, all wicked glee.

Peter stared at them for a moment. "You're putting me on," he said finally. The girl shook her head with total sincerity. "My God. Young lady, your friend needs a police psychologist, not a vampire hunter."

"Please, Mr. Vincent," she started to plead.

"I'm afraid not, my dear. You see, Hollywood beckons. I've been offered the starring role in a major motion picture. I've even had to retire from *Fright Night*, so—"

"You're kidding!" the boy exclaimed. He looked suddenly crestfallen. It warmed Peter's heart.

"I'm afraid so. Why? Are you a fan of the show?"

"Since day one," the boy replied unhappily.

"Oh, my goodness," Peter purred. "Well, we certainly can't let you get away without an autograph, can we?" He started to rummage through the papers on his desktop in search of a pen.

"Mr. Vincent. Please." The girl's voice had taken on a sudden, sharper tone. He turned to her, startled.

"I'll hire you," she concluded. "I'll give you money."

"How much?" Peter interjected, quick as a wink.

"Five hundred dollars."

"I'll take it."

Peter Vincent's entire being transformed at the sound of those three magic words. *Five hundred dollars*. He could pay the rent and hold off the phone company, give himself time to find a new base of operations. There was a station in Cleveland that had expressed interest in him; God only knew how many other Saturday-night horror shows needed hosting by someone with his obvious gifts.

"So how do we go about curing your little friend of his delusion?" he began, all jolliness and willingness to help.

"I've got it all figured out," the boy said. "We all go over to his neighbor's house and run a little vampire test on him. You know, like in *Orgy of the Damned?*"

"Ah, yes!" Peter was positively glowing now. "Would you believe that I still have the prop?" He reached into the vest pocket of his smoking jacket and pulled out a silver cigarette case. He flipped it open, revealing the white filter tips of his Carlton 100's and the inside of the lid.

A mirror.

"You see?" he said, displaying it to Amy. "Most vampires don't have mirrors in their homes. It would be a bit disconcerting, I'd imagine, to try to catch a glimpse of yourself and find nothing there." He chuckled, flipped the case shut and put it back in his pocket. Then he turned to the boy and said, "It sounds fine to me, but has the neighbor agreed?"

The boy grinned. "I'll take care of it. Umm... may I use your phone?"

Peter Vincent was more than happy to show him the way. The magic words were still high-stepping like chorus girls through his mind. He could scarcely imagine a more joyous piece of synchronicity.

All the clocks started ticking at once. The great grandfathers, the equally antique wall and desk models, all burst into perfectly synchronized motion.

Precisely at six o'clock.

In the front parlor, Billy Cole finished munching the last of his toast, took one final sip of tea and folded the newspaper neatly on the tray. He smiled, the tiniest flit across his features, as he glanced at the lurid headline:

RANCHO CORVALLIS KILLER STRIKES AGAIN
NUDE COED SLAUGHTERED
Details, pg. 3

Billy picked up the tray and made for the kitchen. His mind held only happy thoughts...

... Her name was Jeanette, and she really was a college student (or so she said), and she didn't do this very often but she needed the money for the spring semester (student loan cutbacks, she said)... She was petite, but her breasts were very full and lush, they pressed against her bare forearm as he slipped the bag over her head and trundled her into the Jeep... She was still alive then, just barely, but no matter; it was a long drive to the quarry and he'd go slow. By the time he got there she'd be cooling and just right...

... Then he'd have his fun...

He puttered around the kitchen, tidying up. Dandrige insisted the place be kept spotless. *But not so bad, this work,* he mused. *Where else can one enjoy such delicacies?*

Just short of 6:10, the phone began to ring. By that time, footsteps were already coming up the steps.

Billy moved to the phone and picked it up, said "Yes?" into the receiver.

A moment passed, and Jerry Dandrige appeared at the top of the basement steps. He looked well-rested. He looked perfect, as usual.

"It's for you," Billy said.

Jerry nodded, entering the kitchen. He almost seemed to *glide* across the floor, though Billy knew that wasn't exactly the case. It was just the unbelievable grace of their kind. For a second, he envied his master, then quickly clamped a lid on the thought. His role was different, by necessity. Their powers would never be his.

His powers were enough.

Jerry nodded politely and took the phone. "Yes?" he said pleasantly. Billy stepped back into the shadows and waited.

The master nodded, made little noises of amusement and agreement. It went on for about thirty seconds. Then he cleared his throat and said, "I see. Yes, of course. I'm always willing to help young people. But I'm afraid that the crosses just won't do. You see, I've recently been born again..."

He grinned at Billy. Billy smiled back.

"Yes, exactly. I will not have the sacraments taken lightly in my presence. I must be very firm about that. My faith demands it."

A second's pause. "Yes, I'll hold on." A longer pause, followed by the little noises again.

"Fine," he said finally. "As long as the water's not sanctified, I see no harm in getting splashed a little. No problem at all."

Another pause.

"Actually..." he said, drawing it out, "this evening would be perfect. We had a previous dinner engagement, but unfortunately, it's been cancelled. A visit from you and Mr. Vincent would be wonderful. Please come... Oh, yes. Bring the boy and his girlfriend with you."

Billy began to chuckle. Jerry waggled a finger at him, but the gesture had no authority. The master was desperately trying to keep from laughing, too.

"Yes, yes. Fantastic. An hour will be fine. I'll see you soon... No, no, thank *you*! 'Bye!"

He hung up the phone, and they looked at each other in the darkened living room. Billy shrugged and grinned, as if to say *Don't ask me, Boss. I only work here.*

"You know something, Billy?" the vampire said at last. "Sometimes I think that somebody up there likes me." He pointed a long, bony talon toward the heavens.

Then they laughed, and they laughed, and they laughed.

"All set," said the boy. "Now all we've got to do is get Chucko to join us."

"I'll take care of that," the girl announced. She cast a slightly cold gaze at Peter and added, "If I might use your phone, now."

"By all means," Peter gushed, motioning her forward with a sweeping gardyloo. He recognized the expression on her face: the resentment, the grudging dependence, the godlike aloofness that came with holding the purse strings.

No matter, he thought as she began to dial the number. *I doubt very seriously that I'll have to put up with five hundred dollars' worth of malevolent glances.*

He had no way of knowing how entirely wrong he was.

Fourteen

Three studies in agitation: one contemptuous, one compassionate, one complete.

"It's seven-oh-five," Charley noted, somewhat twitchily. "He said seven, right? So where is he?"

"Don't get your undies in a bundle, Chucko. The man said he'd be here. He'll *be* here, fercrissakes." Eddie turned and thrust his hands into the pockets of his flight jacket. "He better, for all the cash she's dishing out."

Amy kicked him, subtle yet hard. Charley paid no attention, utterly lost in his thoughts. "He'll be here," she said, touching her boyfriend's shoulder gently. "I promise."

Charley was about to respond from his bottomless pit of doubt when he saw the ancient Rambler chugging up the street. "He's here! All right!" he yelled, rushing forward to meet it. Amy and Ed shrugged and fell in behind.

"He *is*?" Eddie was a little taken aback by the Great Vampire Killer's seedy transportation. He expected a little more show for that much dough, even if it was somebody else's.

The Rambler pulled up, shuddering to a stop. Charley bounced up and down like a cocker spaniel, scarcely able to contain himself. "Mr. Vincent, I can't tell you how much I appreciate this."

Peter Vincent climbed out of the car. He was dressed in full vampire-hunting regalia: a Victorian

Harris Tweed suit, complete with mackintosh and cap. He shook Charley's hand earnestly, laying it on with a trowel. "Not at all. Terribly sorry about our encounter this morning, but you must understand that I get similar requests constantly, and not all are as well founded as your own." He looked at Amy. She smiled approvingly.

"But when your friends here explained the direness of your plight, it was clear where my duty lay. So," he concluded, clicking his heels and bowing curtly, "Peter Vincent, Vampire Killer, at your service.

"And now, down to business. Where is the lair of this suspected creature of the night?"

Charley pointed nervously. "Right there," he said.

Peter studied the house gravely. "Ah, yes. I see what you mean. There *is* a distinct possibility." He reached into the car, withdrew a small leather satchel. Placing it upon the hood of the car, he opened it, removing a delicate crystal vial of liquid. Then he put the bag back and turned to the kids, straightening his shoulders. "Well," he said, "shall we go?"

Evil Ed snickered a tiny bit. "Where're your stakes and hammer?"

Peter Vincent regarded him coolly. "They are in the car."

"You're not going in there *without* them!" Charley was horrified. "That'd be *suicide!*"

"I have to prove that he's a vampire before I kill him, Charley."

"But I already *know* he's a vampire!"

"But *I* do *not!*" Vincent leveled him with his most paternal gaze. "Trust me, Charley. I've been doing this for a long, long time, and I'd surely not endanger you, no less myself."

Vincent held the vial up to the light. "This," he said, "is holy water. Duly sanctified and blessed. If he so much as *touches* it, it will blister his flesh. I am going to ask him to drink it."

96

"He'll never agree to it! He'll kill us all!" Charley cried. He stared at the three of them, looking for a trace of sanity.

Evil Ed cackled. "He already agreed, you cluck!"

Charley looked at Peter Vincent. "He *did*?"

Peter nodded gravely. "Yes," he said. "Which doesn't exactly strengthen your case, does it? Now, shall we go?"

Charley was stymied. "But..." he stammered, grabbing Peter's arm.

Amy interceded. "Mr. Vincent," she said, eyes imploring. "If Charley's right, and you *prove* he's a vampire, are we in any danger?" Charley nodded, emphatically endorsing the notion.

"Not at all, my dear. Vampires are cunning above all, and our joint demise would be most difficult to hide." He looked at Charley. "No, we'll be safe tonight, and we can always return to dispatch him by light of day.

"And, after all," he added, winking, "I *am* Peter Vincent."

The actor turned with a flourish and strode manfully up the walk. Charley looked at Amy. Amy looked at Eddie. Eddie smiled and looked slightly askance at the whole thing.

"You pays yo' money and you takes yo' chance..."

They hurried up the walk.

And King Street slipped from twilight into darkness.

Fifteen

The huge oak door opened with a creak the instant before Peter Vincent's hand reached the knocker. He recoiled ever so slightly, as did Eddie and Amy. Charley almost had a heart attack. But the terror subsided as Billy Cole appeared with a sponge soaked in Murphy's Oil Soap from behind the door. He smiled broadly, dropping the sponge into a bucket and wiping the hand on his jeans.

"Oh, hi! We weren't expecting you so soon. Hope I didn't scare you." He gestured at the bucket. "Just doing a little restoration and maintenance. I'm Billy Cole." He extended his hand warmly. "And you must be..."

"Peter Vincent, Vam—" He caught himself. "Peter Vincent."

"Mr. Vincent, a pleasure. Jerry mentioned you." He gestured expansively. "Please, won't you all come in? Don't mind the clutter."

He stepped back and they entered, Charley ducking slightly as they cleared the lintel, as if anticipating an ambush. Amy winced in embarrassment.

Billy showed them into the great hall, the stairway sweeping up before them. To the left lay the front parlor. The wailful of clocks ticked in mad staccato.

"It really is a mess," he confessed. "We just moved in." He turned to the stairs and yelled, "Hey, Jerry! We've got company!"

They waited in rapt silence. Several seconds passed.

"Perhaps he didn't hear you," Peter Vincent offered apologetically. He felt supremely embarrassed. Even the girl's money wasn't worth this ludicrous charade. Damn the fool boy and his cow-eyed sweetheart. He had *some* pride left. Next, he'd be hosting birthday parties.

Billy Cole just beamed like a jack-o'-lantern. "Oh, he heard me, all right!"

Jerry Dandrige descended from the darkness at the head of the stairs, the epitome of poise and charm. Everything about him reeked of understated elegance: his shoes obviously handmade and very expensive, his clothes (a handsome wool sweater-and-slacks combo) casual yet rarefied. His demeanor was well-bred and almost noble, as if he had not a worry in the world and, as such, could afford to be gracious.

Eddie and Peter were impressed to distraction.

Charley thought him more intimidating than ever.

Amy thought he was gorgeous.

All eyes upon him, Jerry reached the bottom of the stairs and turned to Peter with a blinding smile. "Ah, Mr. Vincent, so good of you to come. I've seen all of your films and found them *very* amusing." He extended his hand.

Peter shook hands, quite flustered. To the best of his knowledge, it was the first time anyone over the age of fifteen had ever admitted to seeing all of his films, much less to liking them. "Why, thank you..." he stammered.

"And who might these two attractive people be?"

Peter beamed. "This is Ed Thompson, and this is Amy Peterson."

Jerry bent low and kissed Amy's hand. "Charmed," he crooned. She looked imminently orgasmic. Then he looked up at Charley with a wink and wicked smile. "That's what a vampire is supposed to do, eh, Charley?"

The whole room laughed. Even Amy stifled a giggle. Charley felt like week-old sheep dip. He glowered and said nothing.

Jerry smiled and gestured to the front parlor. "Please, come in. Be comfortable." He ushered Peter into the living room. Billy followed, laughing heartily. Amy and Ed stared after them, totally captivated.

"God, he's neat," Amy sighed. She practically floated into the room, all but oblivious to Charley's presence. Eddie shot him a disgusted glance.

"Some vampire, Brewster," he said, and sauntered off to join the others.

He would have sent a live grenade in his place if he'd had one. He wanted to scream. *I can't believe you're falling for this snow job!* But they were. It was one paranoid teenager against Vlad the Impaler, and he was losing in a big way.

Got to play along, he thought. *Catch him unawares.*

He made his way into the parlor, entering with roughly the fanfare reserved for a wayward family pet. His face looked like he'd dipped it in vinegar, but no one seemed to mind. They were too absorbed in Dandrige's witty repartee.

The parlor was spacious and airy, even though its floor space was crammed with boxes and cartons, all draped with heavy sheets. Jerry looked at them apologetically. "You'll have to excuse the mess. I'm still unpacking."

Peter nodded sympathetically. Charley couldn't stand it. He glared at Dandrige, trying hard to sound tough and resolute. "Where do you keep your coffin? Or do you have *more* than one?" The words came out a petulant whine.

"Charley..." Peter growled, trying to conceal his anger.

Dandrige remained unruffled. "It's all right, Mr. Vincent. As you may have noticed, I am rather fond of antiques," he said, gesturing around the room. "In fact, it is the means by which I made my fortune: dealing in antiques and *objets d'art*. The 'coffin' which apparently started this entire affair is actually a sixteenth-century Bavarian chest that Charley saw Billy and me carrying in."

"That's right," Billy chimed in. "Jerry finds 'em, I fix 'em up. We're partners."

"Bullshit," Charley said. "It's all bullshit! It wasn't a chest, it was a coffin! And he's not your partner, he's your *master!* I saw you on your *knees*—"

"CHARLEY!" Peter was aghast. *I was right. He's completely insane.*

"Quite all right, Mr. Vincent," Jerry said. "I'm used to it by now. As you may know, Charley even brought the police here yesterday."

Peter winced. That was it; he wanted out of the entire mortifying situation. Let the kid talk to his mother, or a psychiatrist, or Phil Donahue, for all he cared. The *police?*

Everyone stared at Charley as if he'd just had an accident on the rug. *Bad, Charley! Bad, bad, bad, bad...*

"Oh, Charley, you *didn't*..." Amy looked shamefaced.

"Damn right I did!" he said emphatically. "Only the cops didn't believe me any more than you do." He stared at Amy, then turned to Peter and said, "But you will. Mr. Vincent, give him the holy water."

"Charley, there's no reason to be rude about this," Peter said, smiling through gritted teeth.

"No, Mr. Vincent, he's quite right. Where is the, ah, *holy* water?"

Peter withdrew the vial furtively. Ed's eyes twinkled. "Are you *sure* that's holy water, Mr. Vincent?" he chided.

Peter smiled, nodding confidently. "Positive," he said. "It's from my personal cache. Father Scanlon down at Saint Mary's blessed it personally." He handed the vial to Jerry, who accepted it with a faint reticence.

Jerry searched Peter's eyes briefly. The old bugger was a nutcase, most certainly. *Did* he have a stash of holy water? He was so absorbed in his pitiful persona, he just might. If it *was*, to even touch it to his lips would mean ceaseless searing agony.

He uncapped the vial, sniffing for any trace of danger. All eyes were glued to his movements. Billy quietly stepped back, moving to block the portico doorway. The tension was a palpable presence in the room, the air tinged with electricity.

Charley edged closer to Amy, simultaneously sliding the cross from his pocket. *"Get ready to run,"* he whispered. *"I'll protect you with this."*

Jerry smiled and shrugged, tipping the vial back into his mouth. He drained it in one gulp. Winked. Bowed with a flourish.

And all hell broke loose.

It happened very quickly. Dandrige doubled over suddenly, breath rasping in horrible dry heaves. Amy, Peter and Ed rushed forward. Charley reared up triumphantly, brandishing the cross. Before he could speak, a large hand wrapped his and squeezed, snapping the cheap crucifix in two. He turned to face Billy, who was smiling and shaking his head.

And above it all, laughter.

Dandrige straightened, laughing heartily. Shock, relief, and confusion flooded his guests. Billy laughed, clapping Charley on the back. The whole room resounded with the revelry of the prank.

All, save one.

"That, too, is what a vampire's supposed to do. Isn't it, Charley?" Jerry said.

Peter turned to Charley, infinitely grateful to Dandrige for deflecting the embarrassment from himself. "You saw it. Are you convinced now that Mr. Dandrige is not a vampire?"

Charley felt likely to explode. "It's a TRICK! It must be! The water wasn't blessed right, or it wasn't blessed at all!"

"Are you calling me a *liar*, young man?" he said huffily. "You have already embarrassed yourself once tonight. I see no reason to compound the error."

"Yes, Charley," Dandrige said. "You've already caused your friends quite enough pain. You don't want to cause them any more, now, do you?"

Charley averted his eyes, miserable in his defeat. *Sonofabitch has me locked up tight*, he thought. *They'll never believe me now.*

"I guess not."

"Excellent." Jerry smiled as the tension flowed out of the room. "I'm so glad that this is straightened out at last." He gestured, arms wide, ushering them to the door.

Billy turned to Peter. "I'll get your coat," he said, moving toward the antechamber.

At the door, Jerry turned to Amy and Ed. Billy returned with Peter's coat, helped him into it. Peter reached into his pocket for a smoke, feeling vastly relieved.

"It's been very nice meeting both of you," Jerry said, "despite the peculiar circumstances. Please don't be strangers." He singled Amy out, his eyes flashing ever so slightly. "You'll always be welcome."

Her eyes clouded momentarily, as the seed took root.

(Say "thank you.")

"Thank you," Amy replied, staring blankly.

("I'd like that")

"I'd like that, Mr. Dandrige..."

"Please. Call me Jerry."

(Kiss, kiss.)

"And you," he said, turning to Eddie...

Peter tamped his cigarette on the mirror inside his case. A few shreds of tobacco fell out onto the mirror. He leaned forward slightly to blow them away.

And his blood froze in his veins.

He couldn't believe his eyes. There they were: Charley, looking sullen and impatient; Amy, staring dreamily into space...

And Ed, heartily shaking hands with the thin air before him.

Peter looked up. There was Dandrige, all effluent grace.

He looked down. No Dandrige.

Dandrige.

No Dandrige.

Peekaboo.

Peter Vincent, the Great Vampire Killer, went pasty with shock. The case fumbled and fell to the floor with a crash and a tinkle of shattered glass. He knelt, heart pounding, and scooped up the wreckage.

All eyes turned to him. Peter whisked the case off the floor and into his mack before anyone had a chance to see what it was.

"Something wrong, Mr. Vincent?" Dandrige asked, conciliatory.

"No, no, just my own clumsiness," Peter stammered. He hoped that his shaking wasn't obvious to all. "Amy, Ed, Charley, we've taken up quite enough time. Come along."

Jerry watched the old fart advance toward the door. He looked ashen, shaky. Palsied. He wondered if the man was having some sort of seizure. Peter turned to him, eyes wide, smiling stiffly.

"Thank you once again, Mr. Dandrige. Mr. Cole." Polite nods.

"My pleasure. Please, come back anytime."

Peter Vincent nodded curtly and practically fell out the door in his haste to depart. The kids followed suit, Charley throwing one last baleful glance into the room. Billy shut the door quietly after him, smiling a tiny and humorless smile.

"Bravo," he said. "A faultless performance."

Jerry strode down the hall, stopped suddenly to scoop up something bright. Something shiny. He turned it over and over in his hand, then held it up for

105

Billy to see. His comprehension grew with every refraction of light that played off the surface of the mirrored glass.

"Perhaps not," he mused aloud.

Peter made it to his car in record time. It would have been unseemly to run, but there was nothing wrong with walking just as fast as his scrawny legs would carry him.

Charley was completely confused. *He acts like he's gonna have a goddam coronary.* "What's wrong with you?" he asked.

"Nothing. Leave me alone." Peter was leaning against the car door, fumbling for his keys. His breath came in ragged clumps.

"Then why are your hands shaking?"

"They are *not* shaking. Now leave me alone, I say!" He dropped his keys, flustered.

"You *saw* something back there, didn't you?" Charley said accusingly. He pointed back to the house. Amy and Ed were just leaving the porch.

Peter glared at him. "I saw nothing," he said. "*Nothing.*" He put his key in the slot, engaging the lock, then threw the door open and slid behind the wheel.

"You saw *something*," Charley said, his voice drowned out by the gunning of the Rambler's engine. "You saw something that convinced you that he's a vampire, didn't you?"

"No!" Peter threw the car in gear, grinding the clutch.

"DIDN'T YOU?"

"PISS OFF!"

The Great Peter Vincent stomped on the gas, tires squealing as he roared off into the night.

"Shit!" Charley muttered, stomping his own foot on the ground. "Shit, shit, shit, shit, shit..."

Sixteen

Charley was very intense, Amy thought. Clearly, the meeting had failed in its primary purpose; he still believed that Jerry Dandrige was a vampire. He hadn't stopped arguing with Evil Ed about it, in fact, for the last twenty minutes, ever since they'd started walking Amy home.

She felt curiously out of it, listening to the two of them go back and forth. Her rational mind wanted to tag-team with Eddie, pin Charley's shabby logic to the mat. But there were dark shapes moving in the shadowed recesses, where thought gave way to whispering hunches and quietly nagging fears. They had kicked the legs out from under her conviction.

They had given her reason, however unreasonable, for doubt.

What if he's right? she found herself wondering. The thought refused to laugh itself away. Something strange had happened when Dandrige had looked at her, that much was for sure. Something strange.

And not altogether unpleasant.

They'd gone nearly a mile already, moving briskly toward the center of downtown Rancho Corvallis. The first of the five- and six-story buildings began to loom above them, sporadically crowding the sky. Green Street was desolate and anything but green: an endless stretch of gray on gray, punctuated by pools of light and darkness.

There was a singularly dark alley on their left. Naturally, Evil Ed moved toward it. "Hey," he called. "Let's cut through here."

"No *way*, man! We want people and lights, the more the better!"

"Yeah, well, you picked the right spot for it, Ace; nothing but people and lights, far as the eye can see!" He gestured broadly at the emptiness surrounding them.

Charley bridled. "Well, it's better than *that!*" Pointing at the alley. "That's a goddam *death* trap!"

"Aw, fuck you, Brewster! You're certifiable, you know it? You're one for the files!" He moved away from the others decisively now, heading toward the mouth of the alley. "I'm splitting."

"Ed, please." Charley dropped his anger, and the only sound left was fear. "Just stick with us."

"Piss off. Amy, I'm sorry your boyfriend is such a jerk. I just can't watch him walk around with a load in his pants anymore. It's embarrassing." Then he disappeared into the darkness.

Throughout it all, Amy remained strangely unmoved. The shadowshapes were crowding more and more of her mindspace, taking her farther and farther away from Green Street, Charley and Ed, the endless argument. She didn't resist when Charley took her by the arm and said, "Forget it. Dandrige wouldn't want him anyway. Probably give him blood poisoning."

It was the scream that brought her out of it.

Every hair on her body jerked to attention; her every nerve ending shrieked in sympathetic discord. It was like catching a quick 110 volts from a faulty extension cord: the terror that sizzled through her was a living thing, crackling and burning and fusing what it touched.

Her hands came up to lock on Charley's shoulder in a death grip. Her eyes came up to lock with his. They shared a moment of mutual nightmare paralysis...

... and then the scream came again, louder this time, and worse. Much worse. As if someone had reached down the dying throat, yanked it out, and hurled it bleeding through the air. *Evil Ed, it's Evil Ed, it's Evil...* her mind chanted in crazy singsong...

... and then they were running straight into the mouth of the alley, feet slapping percussively against the pavement. Not thinking about how much noise they were making. Not thinking about how they might as well have been blowing a bugle.

Not thinking about the death that they were racing toward.

Roughly midway down the alley there was a row of trash cans. A few of them had been toppled over *(and hadn't she heard the sound of crashing metal, mixed in with the screams?)*. They lay on their sides, contents ripe and festering on the cobblestones.

A dark shape lay behind them, crumpled against the base of the wall, not moving. Amy grabbed Charley by the arm again, jerked him to a halt, and pointed a quivering finger.

"Oh, God," he whispered.

Slowly now, they moved toward the body. It lay there, huddled, a fetal ball of unmoving limbs. The head was tucked in and away from them. They could not see his face.

"Oh, God, Eddie," Charley moaned. "Oh, God, Eddie, no..."

They knelt beside the body. It did not move. It did not breathe. Amy became aware of the ice water that was trickling into her bowels. She felt light-headed and queasy, close to shaking apart.

This can't be happening, this can't be happening, droned a voice in her mind as Charley reached out tentatively to touch the still shoulders...

... and the body whirled, howling, clawing out for his throat.

Amy screamed and staggered backwards. Charley screamed and fell back on his ass. The body screamed and fell forward, on top of Charley, grappling for his jugular. *"RAAAARRGH!"* it howled. *"I'VE GOT YOU NOW!"*

Then it rolled over on its side, laughing hysterically.

"*What?*" Amy squeaked. She tried it again: "*What?*" It didn't work any better. She had lost her voice; she had lost her bearings; she had very nearly lost her mind.

But Charley was on his feet, yelling, "You *asshole!* You fucking *asshole!*" at the top of his lungs; and Evil Ed was still rolling around on the pavement, hooting and gasping for air. Then it all clicked together.

She started to giggle.

"IT'S NOT *FUNNY!*" Charley roared.

"You... you shoulda seen your *face!*" Evil Ed barely managed to get out among the torrent of *hee hee's* and *ha ha's*. "It was... it was..." He couldn't go on. He was laughing too hard.

Amy couldn't stop laughing, either. It was a hysterical reaction, she knew; it had less to do with humor than with the working off of terror. She had very nearly pissed herself at the time; now she was releasing it in hiccupping laughter, like hot coffee being forced up a percolator's shaft.

"You'll get *yours* someday, Evil!" Charley snarled. Then he grabbed Amy roughly by the shoulder and led her, still giggling, back out to the street.

"HOO HOO!" Evil Ed was in his glory. "HOO HOO! HOO HOO!" It was the funniest thing he'd ever seen, no doubt about it. He wanted to shout after them, soak the moment for a little more comic potential. He couldn't. It was already too much.

What a dope! his mind howled. *What a sap! What a moron!* His sides ached. Tears flowed from his eyes. It was like being tickled, painful and hysterical all at once. He found himself wanting to stop, but the image wouldn't leave him: Charley's face, eyes and mouth forming three tremendous O's of terror, lips peeled back...

Gradually the phantom fingers of mirth lightened up on his sides. He began to breathe normally again. "Hoo hoo," he gasped, the last trickles of hilarity petering out of him. He pulled himself up onto hands and knees, turned toward the mouth of the alley.

It was empty.

"Oh, well," he sighed philosophically. "Can't win 'em all." He brought his right coat sleeve up to wipe at his eyes.

And then the cold hand touched him gently on the shoulder.

"Glad to see you're having fun," said the voice from behind him. A warm voice. Melodious. Oozing sickly sweet mockery.

Ed spun. All the humor squeezed out of him like ketchup from a plastic packet. His breath caught; his eyes stared upward.

Into the face of Jerry Dandrige.

"Hi, Eddie," the vampire said. He wore a palsy-walsy grin. "Good ta see ya. How's tricks?" He made a nudge-nudge motion with one elbow, leering.

Evil Ed took one crab-walking step backward, right into the wall.

"C'mon. Don't be afraid," the vampire implored him. "What are you afraid of? I mean, really. It's not so bad."

Eddie collapsed, curled up into himself. It wasn't funny. It wasn't funny at all.

"I know what it's like for you," Dandrige said. "To be different. I've been different for a long time." He smiled. For the first time, he showed his teeth. They were long. Very long. "I know what it's like to be misunderstood, to be ostracized, to be treated like the enemy."

The vampire stooped, his face coming very near. Evil Ed heard himself whimpering, and was unable to stop.

"But it's going to be different now. Wait and see. They won't be able to beat up on you anymore. Guaranteed. They won't be able to get away with it, ever again."

Very close now. Very close.
Very long teeth. Very long.
And very... very...

Sharp.

"Say good-bye now, Eddie," the vampire crooned. "Say nighty-night. When you wake up, you'll be in a far, far better place. I promise you.

"You'll love it."

It was almost the truth.

But not quite.

Seventeen

There was no scream, only a puny death rattle that barely made it to the mouth of the alley. Charley and Amy were more than two blocks away by then. The only sounds they heard were the staccato slapping of sneakers on cement, the harsh and weary rasping of their breath.

It came to Charley as a rippling in the unconscious mind. It didn't come as words or pictures; it drew no diagrams, offered no explanations.

It did not state specifically that Evil Ed was dying.

But at the moment that the lights flickered out behind Ed's eyes, the ripples began. Like a rock thrown squarely into the middle of a motionless pond, the horror sent wave after circular wave out to stir up the backwaters of Charley's mind. He had no way of knowing why dread washed up and overwhelmed him, made his armpits slicken and tingle, turned his spine into a shaft of dry ice. He didn't know where it came from. He didn't know what it meant.

All he knew was that Green Street no longer seemed even remotely safe. Each corner, each doorway, each sunken recess was a new hiding place for the horror; every shadow was shifting and crawling with death.

And not just any old death, either, his mind thought wildly. *Not just 'now I lay me down to sleep.'* This *is living death that we're talking about. This is rising up to suck the life out of your family, friends and neighbors.*

It wasn't too hard to conjure up images, once he let himself go. It wasn't hard to picture his sweet, bubble-headed mother, giggling in rapture as Jerry Dandrige put two holes in her throat and began to feed. Or to imagine her the next night, eyes bright and redly shining as she snacked on her bridge partner, the blood-stained Cheese Doodles forgotten.

It was just as easy to picture Amy in that situation. Or himself.

Or Evil Ed...

"Amy?" he began, turning to face her, not breaking his stride.

"Me, too," she said quietly. Her eyes told him everything he needed to know.

They started to walk faster. Amy's right hand snaked out impulsively, searching for his left. He didn't reject it. The two hands clutched each other, the cold sweat from their palms intermingling.

Charley was projecting ahead now, on a couple of different tangents. One part of his mind was plotting the quickest route to Amy's. Another was plotting the trickiest route. He wasn't at all sure that he wanted to lead Dandrige to her door. On the other hand, he didn't know where else to go.

He had roughly fifteen seconds to contemplate his options.

And then every light on Green Street went out.

It was like a massive black shroud had been draped over a ten-block radius. The streetlights were out in either direction, as far as the eye could see. So were the handful of illuminated windows they'd spotted along the way.

They hadn't shut off sequentially, *click-click-clicking* down to a vanishing point at the end of the street. They'd all gone off at once. Now only the light of the moon shone down on them.

And the moonlight was cold.

Amy gasped suddenly and yanked on his hand. Charley followed her gaze to the top of the building on their left. A fat ribbon of moonlight draped across its top two floors.

A monstrous black shadow flitted across the moonlit brick.

And from above them came the sound of massive, leathery wings in flight...

"COME ON!" Charley screamed, breaking into a run. Amy was with him, taking off at the first shrill note of his voice. For the first twenty yards, their hands were still squeezed tightly together; then they broke from each other, their arms swinging freely as they pumped every ounce of speed and strength they had into getting away.

They swung left on Rondo Hatten Road, instinctively heading for the late-night section of town. There was a rock club called Lizzard Gizzard's, a country joint called Richie Wrangler's Saloon, and a disco-dancing hot spot by the name of Club Radio. All three were practically within spitting distance... or would have been, if all the phlegm hadn't dried up in Charley's throat.

Romero Drive, Charley heard himself thinking, *is the shit. There'll be people. There'll be light.* He glanced briefly at Amy, sensed that she was thinking the same thing he was, and started to swing his gaze back around in front of him.

That was when he spotted the cause of the blackout.

The lights were out on Rondo Hatten as well, making it hard to see it completely. But there was a light pole on his immediate left, and it had a power box mounted on its side. The front of the box had been ripped off its hinges; the mangled mass of wires inside it dangled like limp strands of shredded intestine.

Omigod, Charley silently screamed, thinking of the power involved with ripping a metal door off its hinges and then trashing a network of high-voltage wires. It was the same power that had plucked the nails from his window frame.

It was the same power that threatened to rule him forever, if he didn't get his act together fast.

Dandrige didn't know the city. He hadn't been there long enough. That was the faith and the hope that Charley clung to as he steered to the right on Wickerman Road, Amy sticking with him. At the end of the block, Romero Drive was in full swing; the power loss hadn't spread that far. He could almost smell the carousing humanity that partied and cruised the center-city strip, looking for action.

They don't know what action is, he mused.

And that, of course, was when Jerry Dandrige materialized before them— midway down the block, in the center of the street.

"*Hey*, you little lovebirds!" the vampire hollered, grinning endearingly. "Care to join me for a *driiiiiink?*"

Charley and Amy screeched to a halt. They were less than ten feet into Wickerman; they recouped half that distance by dancing madly backward, then spun around and headed back down Rondo Hatten.

"*Oh shit! Oh shit! Oh shit!*" Charley whined, in rhythm with his steps. Ahead of them, Usher Falls Road looked even more dank and foreboding than Green Street had. The words *I don't want to die there* flickered across his mind like script from a hyperthyroid's teleprompter screen.

He reached out quickly with his left hand, catching Amy on the sleeve. She yipped like a puppy with a stepped-on tail, whipping her head around to stare at him crazily. "*Back this way*," he hissed, spinning her around. She gave him a slow glance of mute incomprehension, then nodded and began to run with him.

Wickerman was clear as they came back onto it. It remained so as they passed the place where Dandrige had stood. As he ran, Charley kept scanning the sky and the shadows to either side.

No Dandrige. Two thirds of the way down the block, a sudden crinkling and a flurry of motion made their hearts pogo-stick into their throats; it was only a cat, bowling over some wadded-up newspaper. Very close now were the sounds of traffic and boisterous conversation. Still no Dandrige.

We're going to make it! Charley silently crowed. For the first time tonight, he allowed himself a smile. The corner was less than five yards away, the distance closing at a manic pace. On Romero, traffic was moving; he was close enough to make eye contact with the teenagers who leaned out of passenger windows, hooting and whistling at the hordes on the street. Cigarette smoke and exhaust fumes mingled with another scent—higher, sweeter—in his nostrils.

"We made it!" Charley yelled, reaching out to place a hand on Amy's shoulder. She grinned back at him through her teeth, puffing and panting, as they rounded the corner together...

... and ran straight into a trio of tough guys in ragged jean jackets. The lead man, a blond greaser with a narrow hatchet face, had a cigarette dangling arrogantly from his lips. It spiraled crazily through the air as Charley slammed into him, hissed its life away in the gutter.

"*WATCH* it, asshole!" the guy hollered. Charley made an appeasing gesture and slipped past him, Amy hot on his heels. The three toughs turned slowly to watch them pass, debating whether to fuck with them or not.

They didn't have a chance.

Because when Charley and Amy turned around, Jerry Dandrige was there, two feet in front of them, leaning against the storefront window of H & R Block. He met their frozen expressions of terror with open amusement.

"I hope that you two are enjoying yourselves," he began. "Otherwise, this would be a total waste of time..."

They didn't wait to hear his closing boast; they jumped back, as if bee-stung, then whirled and ran the other way on Romero. Midway across the Wickerman intersection, they almost slammed into the toughs again. The sound of bellowing badasses was drowned out by the howls of terror between their ears.

Club Radio was up at the corner ahead. The line out front was tiny, only three or four people; but a group of more than a dozen was closing in fast. Charley and Amy latched onto each other's hands as they sprinted toward the door.

Please, God, make them let us in, his mind cried out. *Please, God, let us make it through the door.* He threw a backward glance over his shoulder and saw that Dandrige was coming at a leisurely pace, assured of his kill. Amy had to drag him forward for a moment, while a ton of black despair settled on his shoulders like a stone.

Then they were running again, Amy now leading the way. They pulled ahead of the oncoming crowd with ten feet to spare, just as the last one in front of them handed five bucks to the bouncer at the door. Charley realized that he didn't have *any* money; he'd spent his last dollar on cheap plastic crosses. "Oh, Jesus..." he started to moan.

Amy elbowed him smartly. He looked up, wincing, then grinned as she shoved a ten spot into his right hand. The bouncer looked up. Charley handed him the ten. The group of twelve closed in behind.

"Thanks," Charley said. He glanced over his shoulder again. Dandrige was close now, cutting ahead of the last three people in line. The vampire looked mildly irritated; the dark glee had been replaced with an even darker determination. Charley looked away, swallowing painfully, and followed Amy.

They took four steps apiece.

Then a massive hand clamped down on Charley's shoulder, squeezing hard. It took everything he had to keep his bowels from letting loose. Only once before had he felt so sure of death: last night, at the window. It was no easier to handle the second time around.

But when the voice boomed out from behind him, it was not the one he expected; and instead of telling him that there was no point in running, it said, "Just a second, little man. You got any I.D.?"

118

The bouncer was a huge black man with a Fu Manchu mustache, a shaved head, and arms the size of ten-year-old maples under optimum growing conditions. At first glance, he looked fat. It wasn't true. All six feet and more of him were packed with some serious muscle.

Under ordinary circumstances, Charley would have turned milk-white if the bouncer so much as sneezed at him. These were not, however, ordinary circumstances. Compared to Dandrige, the black man came off like Garry Coleman playing Mr. T.

And Dandrige was coming, slowly but surely. Charley could almost hear the vampire's voice in his mind, saying, *This is turning into a pain in the ass, Charley. You're going to wish that you'd just given up.* It wasn't true, but it didn't matter; the vampire's face said it all.

"You hear me?" the bouncer asked. His hand on Charley's shoulder gave a vigorous shake.

"Uh-bubba," Charley said. He couldn't articulate the standard underage rap: *I'm eighteen, honest! I left my wallet at home, that's all. I've got my license, my draft card...* He couldn't pronounce his own name.

Dandrige was clearly visible now, less than three feet from the doorway. Somebody was giving him a hard time about cutting in line: a genuine fatso, whose worst threat would be that he'd sit on you. "Back of the line, jerk!" the man yelled, slapping one flabby hand down on Dandrige's shoulder.

Charley watched the vampire whirl. He more than half expected a sudden rain of blubber, like a whale being fed into the world's largest blender. Instead, Fatso just staggered backward, as if he'd just stared into the mouth of hell... which, in a sense, he had.

The whole thing took less than five seconds.

And at the last possible moment, Charley made his decision.

"RUN!" he hollered, dragging Amy by the hand. She'd been standing there mutely, as blank as Charley when it came to plotting the next move. Now she followed, as Charley broke free of the bouncer's grip and ran, not into the club, but away from it.

"Hey!" the bouncer shouted after them. "What about your money?"

"FUCK IT!" Charley yelled back, completely sincere. He was rounding the corner, with Amy in tow. Behind him, Dandrige was just starting to force his way through the crowd.

There was a sudden crashing of metal against metal. Charley spotted a guy in basic kitchen whites, dumping garbage into one of a dozen grimy cans. Charley flashed back to Evil Ed and the alley for a second.

Less than five feet beyond, the kitchen door stood open. Charley and Amy blasted through the doorway before the dishwasher had time to piss or say howdy, much less see them coming.

The cook was quicker. He looked up from his lettuce and started to shout, cleaver waving madly in the air. "Hey, you can't go in there! Hey!"

"Sorry!" Amy called back to him. Charley said nothing. They hit the door that led into the club, burst through it...

... and were immediately assailed by the strobing lights, the throbbing beat and the gyrating clientele of Club Radio.

The dance floor was huge, and utterly packed. Preppies and MTV-style trendies mixed and mingled, weaving in and out of one another to the groove of Michael Jackson's "Thriller." On the four huge video screens that surrounded the floor, rotting bodies clawed their way out of the dirt while Vincent Price did a voice-over that would've made Peter Vincent green with envy.

For some reason, Charley was less than amused. The deeper he stepped into it, the more the whole thing smacked of nightmare surrealism. There was nothing entertaining about animate corpses at the moment; one was following him, and it wasn't very much fun at all.

To his left, on the far side of the room, a small plastic sign was obscured by the glare of the lights. He moved toward it anyway, riding a hunch, Amy firmly at his side.

Sure as hell, there was a corridor trailing off behind the sign. Sure as hell, it led to the rest rooms and a bank of public phones. "All right!" Charley shouted, barely audible over the din of the speakers. "Come on!"

By the phones it was better. He could hear himself think quite distinctly; and when Amy said his name out loud, it cut admirably through the noise.

"What?" he asked, putting the nearest receiver to his ear. He dug a quarter out of his pocket and slipped it into the slot.

"You were right about the holy water," she said with great effort. "It was fake."

"I know." He was punching a number in.

"I just wish that I'd believed you."

"Me, too." He turned to shrug, resigned, at her. "But I don't blame you."

The phone rang. Amy bowed her head in what looked like shame. The phone rang again. Charley turned back to the phone, stared dumbly at the ridiculous plastic fern in its pot by the men's-room door, the tacky stripes that adorned the wall.

On the third ring, they answered.

"Hello? Lieutenant Lennox, please," he said. "It's an emergency."

Eighteen

Peter Vincent sat in the complete darkness of his apartment, afraid to move. His door was barred, bolted and police-locked; pans of water were laid in front of every window; crosses of varying shapes and sizes were strewn within easy reach.

All of this was scant comfort to the great vampire hunter, who sat in his favorite chair munching garlic cloves like breath mints and suffering a severe identity crisis.

Hoping like hell that he would wake up to find this entire incident a simple psychotic episode.

No such luck.

The knock on the door seemed horribly loud, shattering the silence of the room along with the remnants of his tattered bravado. His heart paused a beat or two, as if considering the wisdom of continuing. He swallowed hard, fighting the urge to crawl under the bed and clap his hands over his ears. It took several seconds and a considerable amount of iron resolve for him to answer.

"Who is it?"

The voice came back muffled, furtive. "Mr. Vincent, open up. It's me, Eddie."

Peter didn't move. Didn't speak. Didn't think. His mind was a burning wagon wheel, rolling downhill.

Outside the door, Evil Ed waited with mounting impatience. He pulled the collar of his flight jacket high around his throat, obscuring the twin holes so recently acquired. *Better open the door soon, asshole,* he thought. *I'm starving.* He grinned a horrible grin and tried to sound waiflike.

"*Pleeeease*, Mr. Vincent. Let me in."

Peter Vincent clutched his cross as if it were a hotline to the 700 Club. There was something very strange in the boy's voice, something chilling. It put a wormy feeling in his stomach. He sat up, tried to sound authoritative. It wasn't easy.

"Y-Yes, Edward. What is it?"

"Please, Mr. Vincent, there's a *vampire* out here. You gotta let me in." *Oh, that's rich,* he thought, thinking suddenly of the joke he'd wanted to pull on Amy earlier. It was the one where Tonto and the Lone Ranger were surrounded by thousands of screaming Indians. *"Well, Tonto," the Lone Ranger says...*

The door opened suddenly. Peter Vincent ushered him in with his eyes glued to the stairwell, in fear of sudden attack. Eddie hunkered in, shoulders bunched. Peter shut the door and locked it securely. When the last lock was fastened, he breathed a sigh of relief and turned to address his visitor.

"Well, Eddie," he said. "What are we going to do?"

Eddie turned and smiled, putting on his best Tonto tone. "What do you mean, 'we,' white man?" he answered.

The joke was entirely on Peter. He stared, slack-jawed and blanched as a mackerel, at the horror preening before him.

"Like it? It's a new fashion concept." Ed took a few mincing steps forward, hands on hips. His jacket hung open now, revealing the withered flesh around the wounds, the blood-caked shirt. It was not a clean kill. His eyes twinkled, luminous bulging cataracts.

Evil Ed advanced, still smiling. His teeth jutted like some nightmarish carnivorous gopher's. They had grown quite long in a short time.

Peter's eyes widened. The part of his mind that wasn't busy screaming marveled at this new tidbit of vampire lore.

Evil Ed cocked his head, sensing Peter's thoughts. "Quite the transformation, yes? Bet you didn't know a person could change so quickly, did you? Yes, yes... I bet there's *lots* of things you don't know." He closed the distance slowly, inexorably. "But you're about to find out."

Peter whirled, heart hammering in his chest, and fumbled madly with the locks. The cross dangled from one hand, threatening as a rubber chicken, serving only to slow his escape.

Eddie paused to savor the spectacle of the great vampire killer clawing at the door. It was too much. He burst with raucous laughter, spittle flying from the corners of his mouth. "OOOO! OOOO! Peter Vincent to the rescue! I'm DOOOOOOMED!" He flapped his wrists in a grotesque parody of terror. "*Save* me, Peter! *Save* me! OOOO! OOOO!"

Peter felt the words bite deep. A lifetime of fantasy had coalesced into reality in his very room, and he was unworthy of it. He knew it. Evil Ed knew it.

God knew it.

"I used to admire you, you know," Ed said contemptuously. "Of course, that was before I found out what a putz you really are."

Then he leapt, landing squarely on Peter Vincent's back, hands raking across his face—trying to find his eyes, clear his throat for the kill. The aging actor screeched with terror and spun around, slamming Ed into the door. Eddie kicked and clawed gracelessly, grabbing Peter by the lapels and leaning over his shoulder. The vampire's breath was fetid and chill as he made contact, teeth pressing hard against the soft flesh. An inhuman sound, somewhere between a growl and a whine, filled Peter's ear. He panicked.

And, quite involuntarily, pressed the cross hard into Eddie's face.

It was a reflex action. Peter'd done it dozens of times, in dozens of films. It was always followed by a special-effects sequence, a morass of technicians, tubes and latex appliances.

But the acrid smell that followed was all too real. Smoke curled around the cross, accompanied by the hiss and sputter of burning meat. Eddie screamed like a baby on a bayonet and fell to the floor, clutching his forehead. The voice coming through his hands was piteous. *"What have you DONE to me?"* it cried, and a crazy wave of remorse swept through Peter.

Suddenly, the crying stopped. Evil Ed looked up, fixing Peter with an accusatory stare. Lightly, he traced the wound with his fingertips. And realized, with growing horror, the shape of the brand.

The shape of a cross.

"No..." he whimpered. *"Noooo..."* He jumped up and ran to the mirror, afraid of what he'd see.

Seeing nothing. No reflection.

"You bastard," he hissed. "I'll kill you..." He turned, menacingly.

Peter thrust the cross forward in the time-honored style. "Back," he said.

Eddie stopped dead in his tracks. He winced, unable to face the cross directly. "Shit," he muttered. The sight of it, even in the darkness of the room, filled him with a bottomless nausea. He tried to sneak around it, but Peter was quickly falling into full vampire-hunting mode.

"*Back*, cursed hellspawn!" the actor cried, straight-arming the cross as he advanced. "*Back*, I say!"

Eddie would have laughed if it didn't hurt so goddam much. It was ludicrous. This guy was a clown, *Fright Night* incarnate.

He retreated nonetheless.

This was not good, not good at all. The tables had turned much too quickly, and he was in danger of being cornered. He gazed around the room. Crosses were everywhere, blocking his path. There was only one reasonably clear choice available.

The window.

Peter stared, blank-faced with shock and horror, as Eddie hissed like a trapped animal and threw himself headlong into the window. It exploded outward, fragments of glass and wood showering down to the street.

Three floors below.

Peter stared at the gaping hole where his window had been. The chintz curtains fluttered harmlessly on the night air. From the street below, silence. No screams. No sirens.

Just silence.

As if the night had swallowed him.

He hurried to the window, poking his head out gingerly. The street was empty. If anyone had heard anything, they kept it to themselves.

He stepped back from the window. A life-size portrait of Bela Lugosi in full regalia, long before the Sterno-sucking days of his decline, loomed before him.

Bela had been a good friend. The greatest vampire and the greatest vampire hunter. That painting had been a gift. It was meant to dominate the room. *Bluh, bluh, I vant to drink your blood...*

Peter felt old, all used up. The cross was still in his hand, a smear of goo on one side.

Bluh...

Eddie limped along the sidewalk bordering Badham Boulevard, very much in pain. Foul sweat glistened on his forehead, the kind of sweat found on meat left too long out-of-doors. The brand on his scalp was growing sticky and congealed, stray slivers of glass and bits of crumbled leaf matted in it. *It hurts, it hurts, oh God, it...* The word *God* left a feeling like chewing on tin foil in his mouth. He needed help, bad.

This isn't working out at all, he thought. *Not at all like He promised.*

The jet-black Cherokee pulled up at the corner, and Eddie staggered toward it as if it were Valhalla. Billy stepped out, leaving the motor running. He looked at Eddie with contempt and perhaps the slightest flicker of pity. "What happened to you?"

Evil Ed stood before him, breathing raggedly. "He... he had a cross. He hit me—"

Billy grabbed him roughly by the cheek. "I can see that. Did you kill him?"

Eddie shook his head piteously. Billy snorted, derisive, then grabbed the little vampire by the collar and hoisted him close. "You, my friend," he whispered, "are in the *deep* shit now." And hurled him into the Jeep.

Eddie hit the seat so hard the bars bowed. Billy jumped into the driver's seat, shifted to drive, and sent the Cherokee roaring off into the night.

Nineteen

Dandrige already knew that Eddie had blown it. You don't live that many hundreds of years without picking up a trick or two. He sensed it, even as he strolled through the door of Club Radio. Peter Vincent was still alive; ergo, Peter Vincent was still available to play with.

Fine, thought the vampire, his frail-looking hands clasped together. *It's the chance of a lifetime. I was a fool to give it up.*

He wanted to be staring into Peter Vincent's eyes when The Great Vampire Killer flickered over into eternal hunger. He wanted to watch the transition. Letting Evil Ed do it would have been enough, in one sense—he liked the cast of the horde he was assembling—but turning down the chance to kill Peter Vincent was like passing up a chance to meet the Devil himself; it didn't come up very often, and it was bound to be memorable.

So he would wait. He would maneuver it. For now, he had the nitwit and the virgin to dispense with. They had wasted enough of his time in games not of his own devising.

Now they would play by *his* rules.

He planned to enjoy it.

Very much.

The crowd at Club Radio was bursting with life. Hundreds of bodies swarmed over the dance floor, strutting and swaying to the primal groove. As far as

Jerry was concerned, it was a wonderful thing. He genuinely loved to see people have a good time.

It made them that much easier to hate.

How long, since he had walked among ordinary men and not been a stranger? *How long*, since his last taste of camaraderie with the human race? *How long*, since his last glimpse of the sun? After four centuries and more, the questions had not gone away. Neither had the longings. They had become the worst part of his curse, the source of his only remaining nightmares.

Dying—*real* dying, forever and ever—was something that he prayed for. Killing was something that he'd learned to love. The only real horror lay in memory: of how much he had lost, of how little true humanity remained.

It made him angry, as he thought about it. It made him *hurt*. Most of all, it made him want to find little Charley Brewster and his childhood sweetheart: to quell the disturbance around his quaint new home, to incubate his plague of nightspawn without the glare of the public eye upon him.

He slid onto the dance floor, parting the waves of motion like a shark. His dark gaze went from face to face, searching. Finding nothing.

The ones he sought were not boogeyin' down, which was as he expected.

But they're in here, he thought. *Oh, yes. They are. And before the night is over, they'll be mine.*

The cops had been receptive, as usual. They were receptive to the idea of finding Charley a nice white padded room. Lieutenant Lennox had left word at the desk, and that was as far as Charley got; the desk sergeant dispensed warnings about the joys to be found in Thorazine and electroshock therapy.

Which left him, once again, with the amazing Peter Vincent. Which left him, once again, pressing a phone to his ear while every pointless ring reminded him of how hopeless it had gotten.

Amy was standing next to the cheap fucking plastic fern, keeping an eye out for Dandrige. It was the scariest thing about being back in this little cul-de-sac: short of the bathrooms, there was nowhere to run. He was grateful to her for keeping watch. It let him concentrate on freaking out about the endless ringing.

"Answer me, dammit. Answer me," he hissed into the phone, turning away from Amy and the hallway.

When the monster found them, he didn't even know it.

Amy caught the vampire in profile first, moving through the crowd. He was magnificent, every bit the godlike image he projected himself to be. She found herself marveling at him, even as the flesh began to crawl over her bones.

Oh, God, she heard herself thinking. *How can he be so gorgeous and so monstrous all at once?*

And that, of course, was when he turned and riveted her with his eyes.

It took less than a second. Supernatural vacuum tubes latched onto her will and began to suck away, draining her as she stood. Turning away, pulling Charley from the phone, drawing a bright red cross in lipstick across her throat and forehead: all of her options petered away in the light of Jerry Dandrige's eyes.

It took less than a second of total consciousness and total helplessness *(Come here, you're beautiful, I want you tonight...)* before she started to move toward him.

The phone stopped ringing. A moment of silence. Charley, hanging desperately onto the receiver.

"Yes?" A tremulous voice from the other end of the line.

"Mr. Vincent, please, this is Charley Brewster, you gotta listen to me." A rush of words, no pause for breath. "We're trapped in this club, you gotta come help us."

"I'm sorry." Peter Vincent. In terror. "I can't."

"What do you *mean*, you can't?"

"Charley. Please. You've got to understand. Your friend Eddie is one of them now. He just attacked—"

"Omigod." A sinking feeling, the ton of black despair reprised. *Eddie.* The alley. The voice on the phone.

"—a couple of minutes ago. I was almost killed. If I try to go out, he'll—"

"If you don't come out, he'll kill *us!*" A scream, cutting through the distant dance-floor din. "Amy's here, too, and, omigod, I know that he wants her..."

Tears, threatening to pour. Silence from the other end of the phone.

Followed by a click.

And a dial tone.

... And she was stepping into his arms, the music pushing back the walls as it pounded into her nervous system, galvanizing her into motion that synchronized perfectly with his...

... As Dandrige held her close, hands playing lightly over her back, her hair, the sensations incredible, the abandonment complete, the wet heat in her panties and her heart testifying that she wanted him, she wanted him, whatever he was, whatever he wanted to do...

It was so easy. It was *too* easy, as it had been for what seemed like forever. All he had to do was want them, and they were his. The only challenge lay in the chase itself. The only change was in the scenery.

And in the taste of their flesh and blood, he mused. *Let us not forget.* Over the centuries, he'd become a connoisseur of great distinction within his milieu. He could trace a victim's genealogy back five generations at a taste, pick out the tiniest subtleties of diet and relative health or disease. He'd been the first to publicly claim (to the vampire community) that chemical additives had actually upped blood's nutritional value to the undead: there was something fundamentally *unhealthy* about it that vampires positively thrived on. Ever since, only nostalgia buffs went out of their way to feed on health-food freaks or members of the Third World.

Coupled with his seductive artistry (which was highly rated in that fiercely competitive field), Jerry Dandrige's acute sensibilities made him the toast of the town wherever he went. He was afforded a great deal of independence to go with his acclaim. While most chose to stay at home, maintaining the low profile that their society dictated, Jerry was free to roam and explore in an almost unprecedented fashion; on top of everything else, he was regarded as something of an adventurer. His exploits were legend, even within that legendary species.

And here I am, he thought sardonically, *getting into the swing of things here at Rancho Corvallis's hottest nightspot.* It was a lot like slumming. It really was. If he weren't so fond of the area's flavor...

The girl was grinding against him now. It brought him back to his body, the hunger it encased. Her eyes were rolling back in something like ecstasy, her undulations suggesting the same. It was a reaction he always savored.

Everybody needs a little lovin', a voice in his mind began to sing...

"SONOFABITCH!" Charley bellowed, grabbing Amy by the shoulder and yanking her backward. Dandrige looked up, startled, his eyes beginning to flare up redly.

Charley had picked them out of the crowd, which had parted slightly around them without seeming to know why. Along the way, he'd run into every kind of person he'd never wanted to meet: cranky coke snorters, horny sexagenarians, militant lesbians, ornery Twisted Sister fans. The bar's clientele was a mishmosh of types that seemed to hold no barriers sacred. *Even vampires are welcome,* he'd found himself thinking crazily.

Then he'd spotted them—Dandrige in total control, Amy humping on him like a poodle in heat—and the world had gone a brilliant shade of red. His interior dialogue funneled down to that one polyglot designation, which he repeated as he swung for the vampire's face. "SONOFABITCH!"

Quicker than thought, the vampire's hand snaked out, catching Charley's fist in mid-flight. Pain flooded his wrist, his forearm, the network of nerve endings leading down to his spine.

"You shouldn't lose your temper," Dandrige scolded, grinning. "It isn't polite, you know."

The vampire squeezed harder, pulling him close. The pain became unbearable. Charley buckled and fell to his knees, whining. "You can't kill me here," he managed to say.

"But I don't *want* to kill you here!" Dandrige exclaimed. "My idea was to have you join me at my house. With Peter Vincent, if you don't mind terribly. Between the three of you"—doing a long vaudevillian grind against Amy's still-bucking pelvis—"I'm sure I'll have a wonderful time.

"So be there, if you want to see her alive again." The vampire whipped off a vicious sneer at that point, squeezing even harder. Charley swore that he heard the sound of popping knuckles, but it was hard to tell through the seismographic pounding of the music. He let out a barely audible scream. Tears rolled out of his eyes.

"Up to you, Charley," the vampire concluded. "You don't have much of a chance, but at least it's something. I'd take me up on it, if I were you."

Then the pressure released, and Charley crumpled to the dance floor. Dandrige let out a tiny burst of laughter and turned, pulling Amy alongside him as he made his way to the door.

BASTARD! Charley thought, but he was hurting too badly to articulate it. On the video screens that surrounded him, a were-woman vamped through the woods while the boys from Duran Duran informed him that they were hungry like a wolf. Several hundred assholes shimmied and swayed while his hand screamed bloody agony, oblivious to the nightmare that was going on around them.

BASTARD! he thought again, and then he was running after them, the pain ignored if not forgotten. More quietly, the words *Amy, I love you, I won't let him get you* played subtext to his rage.

And then the massive hand clamped down on his shoulder again.

"*There* you are, little bro'!" the bouncer said conversationally. "We was *wondering* when we would find yo' ass!" Amusement was written all over his face. The quality of mercy was not. "Where's your little girlfriend?"

"THAT'S WHO I'M TRYING TO *FIND!*" Charley screamed. "LET ME GO!"

"Don't dick around with me, boy," the bouncer assured him. "I might snap you in half."

"BUT..." Charley began at high volume, and then he spotted them: at the edge of the dance floor, less than ten feet from the door. "THERE SHE IS!" he bellowed, pointing wildly.

The bouncer grunted and nodded once. He bowled through the crowd like a leviathan engine, dragging Charley behind him. A second bouncer, shorter and thinner but no less black or bald, gave them the okeydoke sign and moved to block the door.

Both of the bouncers were supremely confident, stepping over the border into cockiness. Charley wondered, for slightly less than a second, why that failed to assuage his fear.

And then all hell broke loose.

"'Scuse me, muh man," the skinny little black dude said. He had stepped away from the door and made his way up to them in the crowd. "I think your girlfriend an' I gots to have us a word or two."

"No," said Jerry Dandrige. He was not in a trifling mood. Getting stopped at the door was not in the script. It pissed him off. It was the kind of annoying diddly-shit that made him wish for his home in

Transylvania, where caterers took the bother out of mealtime.

"It ain't a matter of dee-bate," the bouncer insisted. "We got the Liquor Control Board snoopin' around here tonight. If you wants to grab chicken, you just hang out like a good boy an' wait 'til we're done, or drag yo' ass down to Elvira Boul—"

The bouncer never got to finish his directions for underage meat. Jerry Dandrige had had enough.

He began to transform.

The eyes, first: catlike, slit-irised and utterly inhuman. Then the first protrusion of fangs, contorting the upper lip while the lower jaw bulged and strained. The flesh turned gray and lizardlike. The hair receded, went greasily silver.

He held his right hand up to the bouncer's face, so that the man couldn't fail to see what was happening. Couldn't miss the claws that tore out of the extended fingertips, razor-sharp and gleaming.

Couldn't overlook the last few seconds of his life.

Then the vampire slashed forward, talons raking five jagged grooves across the bouncer's throat. The carotid artery tore with a great sputtering geyser of blood. It jet-sprayed broad strokes of crimson graffiti across half a dozen passersby, spritzed into the eyes of a dancing couple and anointed every drink within a seven-foot radius.

The effect was a smashing success. The screams that erupted were perfectly timed with the Duran Duran girl's first wail of torment. His senses, sharpened by the heady scent of blood in the air, picked it up in Sensurround. Together with the flashing lights, the simple fact that he had an *audience* for a change, it made for one of the most enjoyable deaths he'd meted out in ages.

The dead man was still burbling as he crashed to the floor. The crowd was fanning out around him, still too stunned for a mass retreat. Another black man stepped out of it, much larger than the first. Jerry noted with amusement that Charley was beside him, looking slightly green around the gills.

Watch closely, boy, the vampire thought. He could feel the words impacting on Charley's brain, could see the confusion and terror. *Your death isn't going to be this pretty.*

Then the second bouncer was upon him, towering over him. It didn't matter. *The bigger they come...* he idly thought, pushing Amy gently to one side and then bringing his right hand up again.

Once again, it caught the bouncer at the throat. This time, however, the claws didn't carve. They punctured. The man's huge face ballooned with pain and disbelief. His lips pulled back into a yawning, white-toothed oval.

And the lovely redness began to flow.

"Beautiful," Jerry muttered, entirely to himself. Everybody else was too busy screaming or dying. He liked the dimples in the man's neck, where all five claws were deeply embedded. He liked the way they trickled ever so slightly.

Effortlessly, he began to lift. Over two hundred pounds of limply flailing carcass rose an inch off the floor. Two inches. And more. When the man was well over a foot in the air, Jerry flung him casually into the middle of the dance floor.

Where no one was dancing.

Anymore.

... And the screaming was all around her now, a hurricane howling that shattered her thoughts and sent the sharp fragments soaring through her skull. Words like omigod, Charley jumbled together with help me and so that's what it's like to die, a subsonic morass that drowned in the screaming, but that was strangely okay, because she was screaming, too...

... and then somebody grabbed her by the arm, and she screamed a little more until she realized that it was Charley, it was Charley, and his mouth was moving but she couldn't understand a word that he was saying, she couldn't hear him, she was too busy screaming and screaming and...

... then they were running, everybody was running, the world had become a shrieking madhouse of pandemonious motion, wave upon wave of terrified flesh that pressed against her from behind, pressed against Charley, pushed them forward and into the night...

Charley heard a split-second whistling by his temple. Then he felt the blow, and the world went electric with white blinding pain. He felt his hand fall free of Amy's arm, felt himself begin to tumble.

The first wave of fleeing people plowed into him from behind. He dropped like a stone, and they began to pile up on top of him. When his senses returned, he noticed the pair of enormous tits that were jammed against the back of his head. They failed to cheer him up.

"OUCH!" he yelled. "GET THE FUCK OFFA ME! OW!" The weight was crushing; worse yet, it was immobilizing. Above him, the pile was beginning to tip over, to grow in size, to reach dangerous proportions. Charley got a vivid flash of what being trampled to death might be like. He started to crawl painfully toward the curb.

The woman fell off his back and onto his legs. He winced and let out a thin screech of anguish. His gaze swept out to the street before him.

The black Jeep was there. Its back door was closing. Jerry Dandrige stood beside it, grinning warmly at him. Through the rear window, the back of Amy's head was clearly visible.

So was the face of Evil Ed, whose name was no longer a joke. It leered at him as Dandrige hopped into the passenger seat, and the Jeep kicked into rubber-burning motion.

"NO!" Charley screamed, wrenching himself free at last. He staggered to his feet and began to run after them; but the car was already wheeling around the corner, and he was too late, too late...

Twenty

Peter Vincent was throwing things into a battered leather suitcase. His choices were based on nine parts panic, one part practicality. Shirts, socks, pants and underwear were high on the list of priorities, which made sense. On the other hand, one pair of pants, five shirts, five socks and eight pair of underwear, only some of which matched, did not.

Memorabilia kept making its way in and out of the suitcase. Desk-sized photo frames, housing shots of Peter Vincent with everyone from Roddy McDowall to Ingrid Pitt to a late-model, strained and staring Bela Lugosi; his shattered cigarette-case mirror, a stiletto that shot out a ten-inch aluminum cross (from *Hickies From Hell*, the teenage vampire classic), a trick crucifix/spritzer that used holy water instead of seltzer. He even tried to tuck framed movie posters in, but gave up when *Blood Castle* slipped out of his fingers, spraying shards of glass all over the floor.

The room was a disaster area. Evil Ed's visit had been only the beginning; most of the damage had been done by Vincent himself. Drawers were thrown open and tossed to the floor; the things still hanging on the walls were wildly askew. A hurricane called Hysteria had blown through the room, and nothing therein would ever be the same again.

I gotta get outta here, I gotta get outta here, his thoughts prattled over and over. It was the mantra of a man in mortal terror. A psalm on self-preservation. A communion with cowardice. *I gotta get outta here.* The only thought in his head.

When the knocking at the door began, he let out a little shriek and dropped everything he was clutching.

"MR. VINCENT!" screamed the voice from the hall. "OPEN THE GODDAM DOOR!" The pounding continued, making the fillings in Peter's teeth rattle.

He thought he recognized the voice, but it was hard to tell: he'd never heard such panic. All the same, he edged toward it tentatively.

"Who is it?" he trilled, voice thin and quavering.

"CHARLEY BREWSTER, GOD DAMN IT! LET ME IN!" The pounding stopped, and there was the muted thump of Charley, leaning heavily against the door. Peter put his hand on the knob, started to turn it, then thought better of the idea.

"What do you want?" he asked. "I'm very busy."

"HE HAS AMY!" Charley howled, and the pain in that voice stabbed into Peter's gut like a rabies vaccination. "HE HAS AMY, AND WE'VE GOT TO SAVE HER, AND I NEED YOUR HELP, AND... OH, GOD DAMN IT, JUST *OPEN THE DOOR!*"

Peter could hear, from the other side, that Charley was starting to cry. He leaned his back to the door and took a deep, hitching breath that made his chest flare up for one agonized second. The words *heart attack* popped up in his mind like shooting-gallery ducks, then vanished.

I can't do it, he thought, and the thought made him sick. He hated himself, the cowardice he embodied.

He was powerless before it.

"Go away, Charley," he said, very quietly. "I can't help you. I'm sorry—"

The sudden *SLAM* against the door was full-bodied, and more violent than all of the others combined. It made Peter jump backward, heart thumping madly, hot shame flushing up into his cheeks.

"YOU *BASTARD!*" Charley bellowed. "YOU LOUSY, CREEPING, GOOD-FOR-NOTHING *BASTARD!*"

Peter backed away from the door, heading vaguely toward the bedroom. If he pulled the covers up over his head, and pressed all the pillows on top of it, maybe he wouldn't have to listen anymore. Maybe he wouldn't be able to hear the truth that branded him forever...

"YOU KNOW WHAT'S GOING TO HAPPEN NOW, DON'T YOU? I'M GONNA HAFTA GO OVER THERE, ALL BY MYSELF, AND THEN DANDRIGE IS GOING TO KILL *ME!* AND YOU KNOW WHAT'S GOING TO HAPPEN *THEN*, RIGHT?"

Charley was sobbing wildly between the words. Peter continued to back away, every step getting harder and harder.

"I'M GONNA COME BACK AFTER *YOU*, YOU COWARDLY SON OF A BITCH! I'M GONNA MAKE A *POINT* OF COMING BACK AFTER YOU, BECAUSE YOU *DON'T DESERVE TO LIVE!*"

The sobbing took over completely then. There was one last vicious slam against the door, almost an afterthought; and then Charley's leaden footsteps staggered miserably down the hall and away.

Leaving Peter Vincent, the Great Vampire Killer, to drop to his knees and start crying himself: for Charley, for Amy, for Eddie and for the long-lost Herbert McHoolihee.

But it was already far too late for that.

Twenty-One

Darkness, spiraling upward into gray. Hardness beneath her, also spinning, like a wooden raft caught by a whirlpool's outermost whorl.

In the distance: strange music, driving and seductive, dark and elemental as freshly drawn heart blood. Injecting her with its rhythms. Awakening her to its call...

Amy pulled herself back into consciousness slowly, battling weakly with the swirl inside her mind. Her eyes flickered open, and she saw that it was indeed dark. There was wood beneath her, yes: a hardwood floor, very old.

And the music was there as well. Not distant at all. Just soft. *Insinuating*, she thought, and the word fit just right. It didn't overwhelm, it worked at her subtly.

She liked the music. It fit her mood, which was dark and dreamlike. No jagged edges. No stridency at all. Just a wicked, languid, red warmth that suffused her, washing over and through her, making her curl and stretch and roll over luxuriantly, then stare up at the ceiling with a smile on her face.

"Well, well, *well*, my little precious one," said the silken voice above her. "You've come back to me. I'm so glad.

"I've been waiting."

Fear, as yet, had not occurred to her. She didn't know where she was. She didn't know who had spoken. The end of her life was the farthest thing from her mind.

There were candles in the room. They were the only source of light. *Romantic,* she thought, enjoying the way the shadows flickered across the walls and ceiling. *That's how I feel. Romantic.*

Like something very special is about to happen.

A very special shadow loomed over her suddenly: a great silhouette, long and stark and profoundly masculine. "Dance with me," it said, and a long band of darkness stretched out toward her.

Her memory came back; and with it, her terror. He liked the girl. There was something about virgins that appealed to him greatly. They didn't yet know what they were missing; it was all pent up inside them, coiling, blindly gathering power. When she came, he knew, it would be in a big way.

He looked forward to it greatly.

He did not plan on waiting for long.

She was huddled in the corner now, her eyes wide and pleading. He understood the emotions that were churning inside her; he could taste them in the air, as he had a thousand times before. They were, as *he* was, undying. They blossomed ever fresh, thank the gods both light and dark. They brought their wide-eyed innocence to the altar for sacrifice, never knowing what they stood to gain, or what they stood to lose.

One after the other.

Forever.

Charley was still at the core of it, of course. The vampire wanted nothing more than to make the kid suffer for his pestiferousness: after that scene in the disco, Rancho Corvallis wasn't exactly safe anymore, and he hadn't even finished unpacking. Charley Brewster had definitely climbed to the top of Jerry Dandrige's shitlist, and breaking in the girl was bound to ruin the boy's morale.

But the girl would be fun. No question about it. She would be fun, and she would be delicious, and she would make a wonderful weapon. The combination was unbeatable.

"Amy, I want you," he purred. "Come and get me.

And then he began to dance.

For a moment, the panic was complete and untainted. All other considerations were knocked aside like Kewpie dolls by the fastball of fear whipping through her. She was alone in the room with a creature of incredible evil, and it didn't look like anybody was going to save her, and the fact that she was about to die loomed more enormously over her than the vampire's projected shadow.

A shadow that had nothing to do with the light in the room. Like a mirror, it refused to acknowledge his presence. Dandrige cast no shadow.

Dandrige *was* shadow.

And that was where the moment ended. There was more than just panic; there was more than just terror. There was *fascination*, sick and intrinsically sane all at once.

Jerry Dandriges didn't happen past every day, don't you know. Most lives were filled with perfectly ordinary happenstances: tick tock, seven o'clock, time to watch *The Jeffersons*. Most people never had undead monsters pursue them all over town.

Most people had never been seduced by an individual of such incredible beauty and power.

And that was the other thing that was happening to her: difficult to admit, impossible to deny. There was an aspect of her that was turned on by the dance. There was a longing, inside her, for something entirely outside and beyond ordinary experience. She couldn't help but respond to the hypnotic motion, the eyes that flashed out of the darkness at her.

Those eyes...

They were the source of his power over her, she realized. His gorgeous body, the liquid eroticism of his movements, made it hard to look away; his eyes made it impossible. They glowed at her, a gold luminescence that didn't frighten, but simply drew her in and in...

"*No*," she whispered. He hadn't taken her will this time, made her a puppet that swayed at the end of his strings. He was seducing it, little by little. "*No*," she repeated, more strongly this time.

And then forced herself to look away.

"Oh, Amy," the vampire's voice crooned from behind her. "Don't do that. Here I am, working so hard to excite you..."

"Stop it," she whimpered, eyes squeezed tightly shut. In her mind she could still see him moving toward her, his feet barely seeming to touch the floor.

"Not when we're having so much fun." The voice was closer now, cutting more easily through the music that went on and on and on.

And the terror and lust and fascination all came together like worms in a can, blindly wriggling and squiggling all over each other, with absolutely nowhere to run. The paralysis was worse than the one that Dandrige imposed, because she'd made it herself.

"*Amy...*" A sibilant whisper, directly above her now.

She started to cry, curling over onto her side and into the fetal position.

"*Ameeeee...*" Leaning over her, closer, closer. A gentle, almost etheric touch, sliding over the tight curve of her buttocks...

"*NOOO!*" she screamed, rolling over and away. Her back hit the wall with a resonant thud. She leaned against it, panting, tears streaming from her eyes.

"Aw, come on," he enticed her, coyly grinning. She saw the first glimmer of dimly lit fangs. And his eyes had lost their golden glow; the glow was red now, and brighter. "Don't try to resist me. It's much nicer if you just give in..."

"LEAVE ME ALONE, GOD DAMN YOU! I WANT..."

"Your mommy?"

"NO, *CHARLEY*, YOU FUCKER!" she wailed, her fists tightening. Her streaming eyes were locked on his, but the fight was still in her. "I WANT CHARLEY, NOT YOU!"

"You'll have *Charley*," he hissed, his voice no longer coy, "as soon as I'm finished with you. That's a promise."

"YOU BAS—" she began, moving suddenly to her left.

And then Dandrige lowered the boom.

It got wearying, after a while. Letting her resist him with her puny will was like letting himself get pummeled with a powderpuff. It very quickly lost its charm.

His eyes were not the thing. She was mistaken in that. He could have clamped down on her mind from the next room, if he'd wanted to. In her worn-down state, he might even've been able to do it from across the street.

Whatever the case, he clamped down now, and her whole being froze in its tracks. No more resistance. No more trouble at all. She was just a pliant mass of flesh and nerve endings now; her feelings were the only things that she could call her own.

"Come here," he said, and she rose to her feet: eyes blank, body swaying to the rhythm of the song. Very slowly, she moved into his arms. Very slowly, they began to move together.

... And his hands were on her, cold upon her, sliding over buttocks and back and breasts and brow, tracing lines of napalm-bright desire wherever they touched. And his lips were there, an inch from her own, never closing that tantalizing distance.

She found herself hungering for his kiss.

It was building up inside her. He could feel its gathering fury. Even as she ground herself against him, ardent and animal, a psychic g-spot was being stroked into frenzy.

He knew the feeling well. His every movement was designed to provoke it. Over the next few seconds, it would build and build.

And then he would release it.

Slowly, gently, he eased her head forward to rest on his shoulder. Slowly, his lips peeled back to reveal his long, slender, perfect fangs.

Her neck was exposed. The vein he sought was laid out before him. Pulsing. Inviting. His mind reeled dizzily for a moment, the bloodlust ecstatically boiling up within him.

"*Now*," he whispered. She moaned in response.

The penetration began.

... And he was entering her, two tiny tiny sharp sharp points sliding past the first layer of flesh, going deeper, finding the hot red liquid center and piercing it through, going deeper, going deeper...

... And she started to scream as he parted her, her thoughts going wet omigod I'm so WET *as the thunder inside her swelled up and up...*

... And then he plunged himself into her fully, and she came, bucking and whining and clawing the air, spasms in perfect sync with the blood pumping out of her like ejaculate in reverse, not giving life but taking it, just taking it...

... And the peak went on and on and on, agony and ecstasy in perfect concert, then gradually eased itself down and down as her passion, like her life, drained away...

Twenty-Two

Charley's desperate pilgrimage to Peter Vincent's ate up quite a bit of time, the defeated trek home even more so. It was awfully slow-going on foot.

By the time he got to his house, it was well past two.

He stared at the two houses side by side, noting the contrast that seemed to grow by the minute: his house, so plain and comfortable and utterly unassuming; the other, a hulking monstrosity, pulling in on itself like the eye of a hurricane.

And, somewhere within, the woman he loved.

God damn him, he cursed silently, thinking of the cowardly Vincent. *God damn him to Hell for being such an incredible ball-less wonder. I wish he could have been there, seen Dandrige at work. Then he'd know he had to fight, that there was no middle ground, no way out, no...*

He went on, riffing endlessly about shoving the truth down Vincent's miserable throat, a nonstop internal dialogue of fear and retribution.

He was so absorbed that he never saw the hand snake out of the bushes toward him.

When it grasped his shoulder, he nearly died. His heart pounded up his throat like it was catching the next flight out, and he turned, bug-eyed, expecting to die.

What he found was Peter Vincent, dressed in his classic vampire-killer mode. A very large, very old satchel, all worn leather and brass fittings, was in his hand.

"Peter Vincent," he said, bowing smartly, "at your service; ready to do battle with the forces of darkness."

Charley didn't know whether to faint or jump for joy. He half expected a trilling rush of violins to accompany the announcement. He tried to speak, failed miserably.

"Huh?" he said.

"Well put," Peter said. "My sentiments exactly. Now shall we proceed?" He started off toward the house. Charley grabbed him, pulling back.

"Wait a second," he said. "Why the big change of heart? An hour ago, you wouldn't even open the door for me. Now you're walking face-first into this. What gives?"

Peter drew a long face. "Not everybody has a code, Charley. We vampire killers *do*, and I've let mine lay fallow for far too long.

"Besides," he added brightly, "you can't hunt a proper vampire without the proper tools. And *you* are woefully unprepared. So, *voilà*..."

He opened the satchel, revealing an arsenal of paraphernalia: several ornate crosses, a bandolier of short crystal vials, and a healthy supply of stout hardwood stakes and mallets.

Charley looked at him earnestly for a moment, then reached and pulled out a cross big enough to play racquetball with, as well as several stakes. He tucked them in his belt. He felt like the Frito Bandito.

"What about Billy?" he asked. "He's human. What do we use on him?"

Peter smiled like the neighborhood fence and withdrew a thirty-eight-caliber revolver. Nickel-plated. Charley remained skeptical as Peter held the gun aloft. "Dumdum bullets, Charley. They'll put a hole in him the size of a grapefruit. If they don't stop him, he *isn't* human."

Charley smiled ruefully, shaking his head. "You thought of everything, didn't you?"

"Let's hope so." Peter turned to the house, showing Charley his good side. "Shall we?"

They did.

The portico greeted them, silent as a tomb, the relentless ticking of the clocks underscoring the deep silence. It was familiar without being the least bit inviting. They crossed the vaulted space carefully, determined not to blow it.

They were halfway up the stairs when the voice assailed them.

"Welcome," it said. "My, my, back so soon? I just *love* having people over for dinner!"

Dandrige emerged from the darkness at the top of the stairs, his night-veil completely lifted: eyes, hands, teeth, all horrible.

Beautiful, Peter thought. *Like some dark god, putting in an appearance before its court.*

Dandrige smiled appreciatively, as if reading his mind. "Yes, indeed," he said. "Welcome to the *real Fright Night*. You, Mr. Vincent, are tonight's guest host. And our pesky young friend here," gesturing at Charley, "gets to watch."

Something in the vampire's tone made Peter's bowels turn to jelly. He gulped, his confidence blown out of the water. With a trembling hand, he reached into his satchel and pulled out a crucifix, brandishing it with all the conviction of a plate of soft-boiled eggs.

"Back, O cursed spawn of Satan!" he cried. His voice was a garbled squeak.

And Dandrige burst out laughing.

Charley and Peter were too stunned to be frightened, at first; but the mirth that Dandrige expressed was hardly one they could share. He laughed on and on, until it seemed he might split a seam somewhere.

Then he stopped. Leveled a mock serious gaze at them. And spoke.

"*Really*, now," he said, stifling a laugh. "May I see?"

He reached down, with no hesitation at all, and plucked the cross from Peter's hand.

"Hmmmmm," he said, fingering it derisively. "Shoddy workmanship. Not built to last."

Then he tightened his grip, crushing the cross into tiny pieces, and flung the remains back in Peter's face. "I do believe," he said earnestly, "that you're missing the critical element, Mr. Vincent.

"Faith."

Peter stared as if he had blown a circuit. He backed away from Dandrige instinctively, his feet locked on cruise control. Charley wheeled in horror as he made his retreat, thinking *no, you bastard, you can't give up this easy!* Then the boy pulled his own cross out and thrust it forward, an inch from Dandrige's face.

"Back," Charley said.

Dandrige stumbled backward up the steps, eyes slitting like a cat's.

"Back!" Charley repeated, amazed at how the power flowed out of him. The vampire continued to retreat, unable to stare at the cross in his hand. "We *got* him, Peter!" he cried.

No response.

"Peter?"

He turned to find Peter Vincent almost out the door, his satchel on the stairs where he had dropped it in his haste.

"PETER!" he shouted one last time, turning to face the vampire, betrayal sapping his resolve...

... as a huge hand caught him right in the face.

The last thing he saw was Billy Cole, smiling grimly as he completed the backhand. Charley spun, the darkness rushing up to meet him.

And the nightmare closed in.

Twenty-Three

Running, running, the Dandrige house and its aura of horror receding behind him, the Brewster house bright-lit and welcome as a lighthouse beacon. Peter's thoughts were chaotic, a tangled web of psychobabble that simultaneously wept, pleaded, called the police and burbled in a style usually associated with mouthfuls of Gerber's Strained Beets.

He reached the front steps of the Brewster house and threw open the door. All was silent inside. "MRS. BREWSTER! MRS. BREWSTER!" he bellowed, slamming the door behind him.

No response.

He bolted the door and raced up the stairs, still shouting her name. An open doorway yawned before him at the end of the hallway, dimly lit from the inside. He made for it, breath rasping sharply, footsteps hammering holes in the night.

Judy Brewster was in bed, the back of her head to him, her blond hair lying across the pillow. It looked permed out of all perspective, more like a mop than a head of human hair. Peter rushed toward her, relief sweeping over his features.

"Thank *God*, Mrs. Brewster!" he began. "Your son is in terrible danger..."

"I know," said the figure on the bed. The voice sounded vaguely familiar. It didn't sound anything like the voice he expected to hear. Peter stopped in mid-stride, his heart almost doing the same.

"Isn't it wonderful?" the voice continued.
Then the figure sat up.
And Peter Vincent started to scream.

It was Evil Ed, and *not* Evil Ed. The shape of the face was the same, but there the resemblance ended. The sign of the cross was still etched in gore across his forehead; it was the prettiest thing about him. His features had sunken, gone grayish-white. His eyes were glossed over with what looked like red neon cataracts; they pulsed with a rheumy incandescence that made Peter want to curl up and die.

Four teeth jutted out over Eddie's lower lip: two fangs, misshapen and deadly, flanking a pair of buck-teeth that made him look like a nightmare Mortimer Snerd. He leered, and the wig began to slide off his head: a ghastly striptease, rife with capering nihilist glee.

"Charley's mom had to work tonight," the vampire drawled. He held up a crumpled note, the type designed for tiny magnets on refrigerator doors. "She says that his dinner is in the oven. Isn't that *sweet!*"

Peter started to back away, mewling.

"Couldn't you just *die!*" concluded Evil Ed, and then he leapt from the bed.

Peter Vincent started running, nearly breathless and blind. He whipped through the doorway and on down the hallway, not even seeing the stairway until he passed it, his bleary eyes catching it far too late...

... and then he slammed into a table cluttered with the kind of worthless bric-a-brac that the Judy Brewsters of the world are known to collect. Wide-eyed ceramic clowns and kittens cascaded to the floor, shattering into a million bright and jagged pieces. The table collapsed, two of its legs snapping off. Peter Vincent followed suit, careening to the carpet with the rest of the refuse, pain shrieking from his right hip.

He had only a second to get his bearings.

And then the monster stepped out of the doorway.

It was a wolf, red-eyed and gigantic, with ghost-gray fur and slavering jaws. It advanced rapidly, grinning as it came, supremely confident of the slaughter to come.

Peter looked away. His gaze fastened on a shattered table leg, its summit tapering off into a deadly uneven point. His right hand clasped it firmly, held it out in front of him...

... as the lupine monster leapt for him, springing on its haunches and launching through the air, Peter screamed and closed his eyes, the table leg upright before him, a last-ditch survival impetus that he invested with no hope at all...

... until something caught on the end of the table leg, sinking meatily onto it. An impulse faster and truer than thought made Peter thrust upward with all his might, his eyes snapping open...

... as the wolf-thing howled and flew into the shattering banister, the table leg skewered through its chest, slipping out of Peter's hands and out into the thin air as the beast went plummeting down with all the force of gravity behind it.

There was a sickening thud on the floor one story below.

Peter allowed himself ten seconds to recover from the terror. Then he leaned over the broken balustrade, staring down at the nightmare beneath him.

The wolf writhed on the carpet, surrounded by broken bits of banister, bleeding slightly.

It doesn't have very much blood in it, he mused insanely. *That's why it wanted mine...*

Slowly he staggered to his feet, leaning heavily on the wall. He forced himself to approach the stairs, then descend them, a part of his mind searching out twists that might leave him still in deadly circumstance. *They can turn into wolves,* his mind chattered. *And bats, and rats, and all kinds of horrible things.*

But a stake through the heart ought to do it, he concluded. *If it doesn't, I'm dead, and that's all there is to it.*

He reached the bottom of the stairs and forced himself to turn. It was not easy. He felt very much like a weary old man, sick to death of the endless struggle. He felt very much like what he was.

Then he turned, and his heart dropped into his shoes.

The monster was gone.

Omigod, he mouthed, no wind behind it. He took a tentative step forward, then another. "No, please," he whined.

There was a thin, viscous smear that stretched across the carpet. It led from the spot where the wolf had landed to the shadows beneath the stairs. Tiny, high-pitched whimpering sounds were coming from there. They were not human.

But they were most definitely dying.

Peter moved forward more quickly now: afraid of what he might see, yes, but no longer afraid for his life. There was an alcove, deep as the stairs were wide. He traversed the distance.

Stopped dead in his tracks.

And stared, more in awe than in horror.

The thing in the alcove was neither wolf nor Evil Ed, but something fantastically between. It still had the enormous jaws, the elongated snout, the pointed ears and black nose, but the hair was rapidly receding. It looked *mangy*, in the popular sense of the word: like a monstrous junkyard dog, the many bald patches in its matted fur testifying to a lifetime of endless combat. Its eyes were squeezed shut—it didn't seem to know that Peter was watching—and fat, slimy tears coursed down its contorted cheeks.

But its *hands* were what really got him. They were trying very hard to be human hands, but they hadn't quite gotten the knack. The fingers were gnarled and far too long, with huge bony knuckles that protruded like knots on a tree branch.

They were wrapped around the table leg, which extended a good foot and a half from the center of its chest.

They were trying to pull it out.

"Dear God," Peter said.

And then the monster opened its eyes.

The monster blinked, through tears of pain, at the man who was standing before it. Concentration came hard—the agony was so intense—but something inside it still hungered for him. Pictures of wide-open bellies and steaming intestines kept dancing and swirling through its mind.

It wrenched at the stake that impaled it, yowling. Everything hurt. The universe was one vast howling continuum of pain, with the thing that had once been Edward Thompson nailed directly to its center.

And the stake was not going to come out. The monster knew that now. It was too weak, too surely dead. There would be no blood. No meat. No nothing. Just agony, and more agony, until the bitter bitter end.

That was when the last remains of Evil Ed, the teenage kid who just liked to watch monster movies, came burbling like blood to the surface.

It was trying to tell him something. He was sure of it. Something unmistakably human had flickered across its eyes, then come to rest there; and its mouth was laboring hard to shape nonanimalistic sounds.

And that was the horrible thing. Like the misshapen hands, its mouth was woefully ill equipped for the niceties of human speech. What came out was a pathetic, inarticulate wheezing, death's breath rasping out in a pattern that refused to coalesce.

Peter dropped to his knees in front of the thing, coming closer. It seemed glad that he was doing it. The thought occurred, not so far from left field, that maybe Evil Ed just wanted one last shot at his jugular vein. He kept it in mind, but didn't let it stop him.

There was no malice left in the creature. He believed it with all his heart. The feeling that overwhelmed him now was neither awe nor horror, but a deep and intoxicating *sadness*. Somewhere, under all that nightmare flesh, a boy who had barely begun to live was trying to tell him something before he died. It was not too much to ask.

"*What is it?*" Peter whispered. He didn't know how else to approach it. He was close now, very close; the thing's foul breath weighed heavy in his nostrils. "*Talk to me, please. I want to know.*"

The monster reached out its hand.

There was a second's hesitation, the automatic rearing of caution's head. Then he reached out as well, leaning closer, his fingertips an inch from the dying monster's own.

Pausing there, as it made one last attempt at speech.

This time, Peter understood what it was trying to say.

I'm sorry...

He mouthed the words, and the wolf-thing nodded. There was a long, electric moment in which Peter just stared into the waning light of its eyes.

Then their fingers touched.

And for Evil Ed, the lights went out forever.

The transformation back to human flesh, and beyond, took only a minute. Peter didn't stick around to watch. He was already moving toward the door.

There were a couple of young people who desperately needed his help.

He hoped he didn't have to kill them, too.

Twenty-Four

Dandrige walked into his bedroom with Charley's inert form draped blithely over his shoulder. He threw him to the floor with an unceremonious thud. The force of landing shocked Charley out of his stupor, horror blooming in his eyes several seconds before he regained motor control. Dandrige smiled reassuringly.

"You recognize this room, don't you, Charley? Sure you do. It's my bedroom. I have *lots* of fun in here... but I don't need to tell you that, do I?

"Of course, I've done some *renovating*," he said, gesturing to the windows, which were stoutly boarded up.

Something moved to Charley's left. He turned to find Amy, curled in a fetal position and shivering. Her jacket was gone, her blouse torn and bloody. She looked feverish. Charley whined low in his throat and crawled toward her.

"You want her, you got her," Dandrige shrugged. Charley threw him a hateful glance.

Dandrige winked and grinned. "Anything for you, babes."

Charley cradled her gently in his arms. "*Amy...*" he whispered.

The words died on his lips. Amy was comatose, deep in the midst of a supernatural transformation. Her body shook with tiny, fitful tremors. Her eyelids fluttered, revealing shiny black

159

orbs. Her mouth worked spastically, an infant's urge to suckle, and her hands clawed reflexively.

"*You bastard,*" Charley whispered, eyes clamped shut in revulsion and pain. Then his temper flared up like a furnace explosion, and he screamed, "YOU BASTARD! WHY? WHY HER?"

Dandrige rolled his eyes. "Well, you've been such a relentless pain in the ass that I thought you deserved a *special* punishment. So, you get to watch her change, and then," smiling impishly, "you can either kill her yourself, or you can be her first victim. Isn't freedom of choice a wonderful thing?"

Charley jumped up and charged him like a pro linebacker, all blind animal rage. Dandrige swatted him out of the air as one might a fly. Charley smacked into the bureau and slid to the floor, defeated.

"Okay, kill me," he said, looking up with finality. "Just go ahead and kill me. But, please, let her go."

Dandrige smiled. "How touching," he said. "Tell you what. I'll take you up on that: I'll kill you first, and then I'll let her go."

He paused dramatically at the door.

"Right. Over. The edge."

Then he leaned over and plucked something from the bedside table, tossing it to Charley like he might toss a biscuit to Rover.

"You may need this," he said. "Just before dawn."

It hit the floor and rolled to Charley's feet: two feet long, utterly lethal.

A wooden stake.

"Noooo..." Charley moaned as Dandrige let himself out and locked the door securely behind him. Charley skittered over to Amy, then held her close to his chest, rocking her like a sick baby. The bare skin of his forearm brushed her lips, and she gummed it insistently, tongue rough as sandpaper.

"NOOOO!"

Halfway down the hall, Dandrige smiled. It was music, pure and sweet, to his ears.

Outside, Peter Vincent regarded the Dandrige house with a curious combination of grim resolve, exhilaration and raw terror. The house itself grew more squat and malevolent with every passing moment. The virtual certainty of what fate lay inside left him curiously calm.

As if he had waited his whole life for this, his finest moment.

After all, not every artist gets to face his fear, and his lifelong fantasy, and prevail. But Herbert McHoolihee would.

If he had to die in the process.

He entered the house quietly, not exactly sure where to begin. At the end of the hall, the door to the basement steps stood ajar. Muffled voices came from below. Turning, he ascended the stairs, his footsteps muffled by the thick oriental runner.

He paused at the landing, staring at the enormous stained-glass portal that dominated the stairway. It was darkened now, its colors muted. But soon—he glanced at his watch, four o'clock—the sun would filter through, showering the room with color.

He hoped he'd live to see it.

The upstairs hallway, too, was darkened, lit only by streetlights that filtered in through windows at either end. He tiptoed along, gingerly twisting each doorknob, his heartbeat thudding in his chest.

The fourth one was locked. "*Charley?*" he whispered, knocking ever so gently.

Charley looked up. "Peter?" he said softly. "Peter?"

"Yes," came the muffled voice from the other side.

"Peter, I've got Amy. She needs help. Get me out of here."

A moment's pause.

"Peter?" *My God, if anything's happened to him...*

"Charley, I'm going to have to break down the door. Make as much noise as you can. Scream. Smash things. Do whatever you can."

Screaming and smashing things won't be hard, he thought. *All I have to do is look at Amy.*

"Okay," he said.

Downstairs, Jerry and Billy busied themselves in the basement. They emptied out a packing crate and spread a thin layer of dirt from Jerry's coffin inside it. This they mixed with a thicker layer of local soil.

Rancho Corvallis soil. For Amy.

Billy looked at Dandrige gravely. "Dear me," he said. "I do hope that she's a local girl." Dandrige broke up laughing, and Billy joined in, their glee punctuated by a faraway sound.

The sound of screaming.

They paused in the midst of their preparations. The vampire smiled a sweet, chilling smile, nodding up the stairs.

"I believe someone is waking up," he said.

Peter considered himself very fortunate that the lock gave out on the first try, as his shoulder felt certain to give out on the second. Real wooden doors were considerably more formidable than their cinematic counterparts, and his shoulder throbbed as he approached Charley.

On the floor, Amy was curled into a full fetal position, her body twitching and slick with sweat.

Charley's voice trembled with ill-concealed panic. "He bit her, Peter. She's *changing.* What are we gonna do?"

Peter knelt over her like a medic giving triage. He pulled back her eyelid, revealing the first traces of red in her swollen iris. Her lips skinned back in a hideous rictus, her incisors veritable fangs now. Her breath smelled like sump water, flecks of foul spittle collecting in the corners of her mouth.

He reached into a secret pocket in his cloak, withdrawing a small vial. Uncapping it, he looked at

Charley and said, "Hold her head. We've got to get her to swallow some of this."

Charley regarded the vial warily. "What's that?" he said. "It looks like more of your bogus holy water."

Peter shook his head, intent on Amy. "This is real," he said. "Now, hold her tightly. She may react quite violently."

Charley nodded and placed his hands firmly on either side of Amy's face. Peter brought the vial to her lips carefully. Every muscle in her body went rigid. Steeling himself, he tilted the vial back.

Amy exploded in a fit of blind panic, lashing out wildly in every direction. She caught Charley with a backhanded glancing blow that sent him careening into the end table with a crash. Peter leapt back, barely avoiding the hand that clawed at his eyes.

And dropping the vial in the process.

The blessed water leaked harmlessly onto the carpet, leaving a small wet spot. Amy spun wildly about on her hands and knees, seeing nothing, hissing like a lizard.

And placed her hand full upon the spot.

There was a shriek, and the sizzle of blistering flesh. Amy fell back, her features contorting in agony, oblivious to everything but her pain. Her mind was a blank thing, a bottomless murky pit, occupied solely by a single word that looped over and over and over...

... and that word was "JERREEEEEEEEEE..."

Dandrige stopped in mid-shovelful, cocking his head to the side quizzically. Billy stopped as well, regarding his master with open concern.

"Something wrong?" he asked.

Dandrige smiled humorlessly. "We've got a visitor," he said.

Twenty-Five

Charley glanced up from Amy's trembling body. She had calmed somewhat, settling back into a whimpering stupor on the floor. He gazed fixedly into the middle distance.

His voice, when it came, sounded miles away.

"Is there anything we can do?" he asked. "Is it too late to save her?" He threw a very pointed gaze at Peter. "*Is* it?"

Peter sighed heavily. "She has to escape the power of the undead, and that power emanates from Dandrige. It's not too late, Charley. Eliminate Dandrige *before* the break of day, and you eliminate the hold of his power.

"But we're going to have to kill him; no doubt, his assistant as well. We've no other choice."

Charley looked at him incredulously. "This is *news?* What the hell do you think I've been trying to *do* all this time? Teach him *assertiveness* training? Jesus Christ! I *know* the bastard has to die! I've known it all *along...!*"

Peter looked hurt and defensive. "But *I* didn't know. And it took all of this to convince me. It's not the easiest thing in the world to believe, and you are scarcely the world's most diplomatic salesman."

Charley stared at him, not wanting to pursue it further, unable to back off. He drew a deep breath and said, as evenly as possible, "Do you believe me now?"

Peter nodded. "Look, let's not be huffy," he said. "There's too much to do, and not much time to do it."

He glanced at his watch. Four thirty-five.

Time enough.

He hoped.

They stepped out of Dandrige's bedroom, melding into the shadows of the hall. Peter moved deftly through the darkness, with well-honed precision (*just like in* Fangs of Night, *when you get right down to it*, he thought). Charley fell in behind, clutching the stake with sweaty palms, as they made their way silently toward the great staircase.

Unaware of the shadows that closed in behind them.

Billy Cole was waiting for them at the foot of the stairs with hands on hips, grinning like the Cheshire cat. Charley wished he would complete the metaphor by disappearing entirely.

No such luck. Billy opened his arms engagingly and grinned a grin all the more hideous for its apparent sincerity. The checkered tiles spread out behind him like an enormous game board (*knight to king four, your move...*)

"Well, well, well," he said, oozing charm. "What do we have here?"

Peter stood his ground. "What we have here, Mr. Cole, is the end of the proverbial road." And with a flourish, he pulled the thirty-eight out and leveled it neatly at Billy's head.

(*Queen to bishop three. Your move...*)

Billy just smiled. "You got *that* right." He began a measured, almost stately walk toward them.

Peter slapped the hammer into half-cocked position. "I'm warning you," he said. "I *will* use this."

(*Your move...*)

Billy smiled on and on. He was five steps away.

Four steps. Peter pulled the hammer fully back. "Stop. Now. Please." Sweat trickled lightly down his hairline.

Billy took another step.

(Check...)

Still smiling. His eyes bored straight into Peter. Another step, almost close enough to reach out and snap his neck like a dry twig.

"Please..."

(Check...)

Billy took the last step, reaching up with calloused hands and taking the aging actor by the collar.

Peter pulled the trigger.

And the darkness swirled behind them.

It all happened in an instant. The pistol discharged with a report that echoed through the hall like a small cannon. Charley felt the tiny hairs on his backside stand on end, as if hoping to somehow migrate *en masse* to his front.

To escape the blackness behind them.

The blackness that thickened and solidified, even as he turned, into the killing form of Jerry Dandrige. Sweeping from an amorphous shadow into the impeccably corporeal Dandrige in one motion of fluid, lethal grace. He moved in for the kill, nimbly hitting the top step.

Arms outstretched.

Eyes, molten pools of slag.

Peter saw none of this. He stood, transfixed, at the sight of Billy, *still* smiling as the vast bulk of his lower occipital lobe sprayed down the steps like so much Hamburger Helper. A piece of his skull the size of a Chesapeake Bay clamshell went skittering across the marble floor with a clatter. The sound seemed to trigger a reaction in Billy's ruined brain. He cocked his head to the side quizzically, as if suddenly realizing that yes, he would be stopping after all.

His eyes glazed over, and he toppled back down the stairs, head hitting the floor with a sound like a ripe melon falling off the back of a truck.

Dandrige roared in outrage as 113 years of carefully groomed and faithful service went careening down to the polished floor, its brains leaking out like oil from a smashed gourd. *Where am I to find another one like him?* his mind screamed. It was incomprehensible that two such incompetents could be causing him so much trouble. This game had quickly turned from mere sport to veritable life and death.

Theirs, or his.

The vampire hissed involuntarily, eyes glossing over, red, and slitted. The transformation mounted inside him, yearning to spill out and slaughter these insects. He held off in much the same way an adept lover might delay the finality of orgasm.

He waited a grand total of ten seconds before the hunger and blood-lust became an all-consuming need. Then he dived for them, screeching.

And came face to face with Charley's crucifix.

"Back off, mother-*fucker*!" Charley exclaimed, straight-arming the cross.

Dandrige halted, dead in his tracks, surprising both of them. He felt an enormous surge of emotion, a coalescence of every miserable ounce of self-hate and misery he had inflicted in the last few days.

All coming home.

Tonight.

Charley felt it, too: a pulsing energy that started somewhere in the center of his chest and radiated out in waves. The vampire had stolen his woman, murdered his best friend, and seduced his mother...

... and tonight he'd pay up. In full.

It was a rare feeling, this.

The feeling of tables turned.

The vampire smiled a sly smile, as if reading his thoughts. "*Are* they now?" he asked. His gaze shifted down to the foot of the stairs, where Billy lay in

168

a crumpled heap. His eyes blazed for a moment, narrowing to slits as he sucked in a sharp breath.

"Yes, perhaps they are, at that," he said, then turned and receded swiftly into the shadows at the head of the stairs.

Charley and Peter stared after him, puzzled at this apparent victory. "What did he mean by that?" Charley asked.

The answer came from the foot of the stairs. Peter and Charley turned in horror to find Billy impossibly, inexorably rising.

Turning.

And coming up the stairs.

He looked up, fixing them with dead, staring eyes. His face still bore a trace of the same idiot grin that he'd worn on the way down. The dime-sized hole in the middle of his forehead leaked as he lurched up the stairs, sending a thin trickle of blood to collect in a pool under his right eye. One hand clutched the banister desperately as he ascended. The other made clenching, circular motions in the thin air.

Killing motions.

Peter Vincent's twenty-five-year romance with the macabre held little to prepare him for the mindless horror of this moment. There were no technicians, tubes or squibs; no one to yell "Cut!" and bring everyone coffee. Life was a cardboard tube; a smoking gun on the one end, a walking corpse with a gaping hole in its haircut on the other.

He brought the revolver up again, leveling it at the Billy-thing's chest.

"God help us," he mumbled, and fired.

The first bullet hit Billy square in the heart, exploding the left auricle on its way out. The second destroyed the superior lobe of his right lung and lodged under the lower rim of the shoulder blade. The third, fourth and fifth scattered about, randomly taking out the left lung, a kidney and his spleen...

... all of which mattered to the Billy-thing about as much as a Congressional Medal of Honor. He was a blank-faced killing machine, running on automatic pilot, as he closed the distance with reflexively clenching hands.

Peter was rigid with disbelief, every neuron in his brain on overload. The delicate fabric of reality was blown away along with any hope in the gun clicking emptily in his hand. He was utterly frozen as the Billy-thing completed its earlier goal, wrapping its calloused fingers around his throat and starting to *squeeze*...

And Charley stepped forward, ramming his stake four inches into the creature's heart.

The Billy-thing relaxed its grip momentarily, allowing Peter to pull away. The actor fell back, choking and rasping for breath.

Then Charley kicked the creature down the stairs. It pinwheeled down, clawing and caterwauling, hit the floor hard. The force of the impact drove the stake fully through its chest.

And the Billy-thing began to decompose.

It bubbled and spattered on the floor, head lolling back and forth spastically, skin falling away in sheets, creating a pool of viscous slime.

In less than ninety seconds, it was done.

Charley and Peter stood on the landing, staring down at the steaming remains for several seconds. Charley grabbed Peter by the shoulder. "C'mon, let's go," he said.

Peter looked at Charley, the shock slowly receding. "He wasn't *human*..." he said, whispering hoarsely.

Charley looked at him in disbelief, then smiled and turned up the steps.

"No shit," he said. "Now let's go."

It was five minutes past five.

Twenty-Six

Charley and Peter hit the top step like a juggernaut, then made their way cautiously down the hall. The shadows seemed alive, undulating patterns of dark on dark that opened inches before them and closed inches after. They moved without speaking, the silence punctuated only by their breathing and their pounding hearts.

The sound of splintering wood cut through the stillness like a knife. And behind it, a woman's cry.

"Omigod!" cried Charley. "AMY!"

He bolted down the hall, Peter hot on his heels. They hit the door like a SWAT team, spilling into the room with near-suicidal determination.

Only to find it empty. One window (the one that faced his bedroom, Charley realized ironically) had been broken open. The heavy boards so recently nailed up had been rudely wrenched off, and now lay scattered about in disarray. Through the window, his room seemed a million miles away.

Dandrige, and Amy, were nowhere to be found.

Peter went to the window, peering out into the night. Charley stood in the middle of the room, waving his cross and stake impotently and screaming.

"YOU BASTARD!" he cried. "WHERE IS SHE? WHAT HAVE YOU *DONE* WITH HER?"

The answer came from further upstairs, as the sound of something landing— something heavy— reverberated down. Peter looked at Charley.

"He's in the attic," he said. "Come on."

The attic seemed fairly typical at first glance. Huge, sprawling gables shrouded in darkness, boxes and crates piled up along the walls. Rodent droppings crunched underfoot. The musty smell of time.

Peter reached inside his cloak, pulling out a small, high-intensity flashlight. He flicked it on, a ribbon of light cutting through the darkness. Dozens of glistening shapes scurried for cover.

Rats.

The attic was filled with them. Fat, bloated little suckers scuttling in the corners, on the crates, over the bundle by the smashed window...

The bundle! Charley thought. "NO!" he cried, racing across the attic. Rats dived for cover, chittering madly.

It was Amy. She lay trussed in a bedsheet, covered with shards of glass, as though hurled through the window like a sack of potatoes. Rats crawled over her prone form at will. She looked dead, or very, very close.

Whimpering, near hysterical, Charley swatted the rodents away with his bare hands. He checked her pulse and murmured her name.

Not dead yet, he thought. *But damn near.* He looked up at the shattered window, then turned to Peter. "God damn him, where *is* he?"

Dandrige hunkered on the roof like a nightmare weather vane, eyes rolled back in his head. He rocked back and forth on his haunches, feeling the tendrils of awareness snake out and down to his seed. His lips stretched back in a grimace, revealing his teeth.

"*Awake, Amy! Awake!*" he whispered sibilantly. "*I command you! Rise!*"

In the attic below Peter cried out. "Charley, come here quickly!"

Charley pulled himself away from Amy, hurried to Peter's side. He didn't notice her eyelids flutter, snap open, bright red.

(Show me how much you love me, Amy.)

Silently, she rose.

(Kill them. Kill them both.)

Peter was standing by the window. Before him was a large, ornate chest. His flashlight illuminated the polished wood, the brass fittings. Charley looked at him. "Do you think it's his?" he asked.

Peter regarded it suspiciously. "Only one way to find out. Brace yourself. We'll have to act fast."

Charley nodded, grabbing the lid. Peter readied his stake, prepared himself and gave the signal. Charley yanked the lid open hard, Peter stabbing down...

... and impaling half a dozen bedsheets.

"Shit," Peter muttered. Charley looked up at him, half smiling...

... and saw Dandrige, hovering impossibly outside the window, one taloned hand reared back and ready to strike.

"Peter, *behind* you!" he screamed.

Peter whirled and dove for cover as the hand smashed through the glass. Charley backed away instinctively.

Right into Amy's outstretched arms.

"*Charleeeee*," she croaked, her voice an insane parody of human speech. She smiled, her lips cracking as they stretched over newly-grown fangs. Her tongue flitted in and out, dry and swollen.

She was very, very thirsty.

"ACK!" Charley screeched. He fell back, stake clattering to the floor, still caught in her clutching grasp. She landed on top of him, scrabbling clumsily toward his throat. Her eyes glowed like foglamps, seeing nothing.

"*Charleeeee...*"

Peter looked up, eyes bulging. Dandrige was nowhere in sight. Quickly, he grabbed the stake off the floor and positioned himself behind Amy, ready to deliver the killing blow.

Charley screamed, *"Peter! NO!"* Amy, still weak from the transformation, smacked her lips in anticipation.

And, from far off downstairs, laughter.

Harsh, mocking laughter.

Sonofabitch, Peter thought. And, switching grips on the stake, placed a well-delivered blow to the base of Amy's skull.

She went out like a light, slumping over Charley's sprawling form. He pushed her off gently, but not without a sense of revulsion.

She smells so rotten, he thought.

Peter hoisted him up. "Thanks," he said, somewhat sheepishly. "You saved my life."

"My pleasure," beamed the actor. "Now let's go find that son of a bitch. We're not the only ones who are running out of time." He turned and headed for the stairs.

Charley glanced at his watch. Five fifty. "Where do you think he is?"

Peter shrugged. "He's got nowhere to go but down."

Charley and Peter hit the hallway, Peter pausing to drop the catch on the attic door. It was not the world's strongest lock, and Peter eyed it disdainfully. "She won't be out for long, you know," he said, "and she'll be much stronger the next time."

Charley nodded sourly, the image of the undead Amy fresh in his mind. He felt queasy at the thought of pounding a stake through her. He felt much better about pounding one through Dandrige.

If he could find him.

They moved along in silence, Charley half lost in thought, Peter a walking bundle of paranoid nerve endings. They were about ten steps from the head of the stairs when they heard it.

Very soft. Very deliberate.

174

"What was that?" Peter said, standing stock still. Charley snapped to, staring at him blankly.

"What was what?"

It came again, so soft one might miss it entirely if one were not attentive. The sound of wood, creaking on brass hinges. Opening, then closing.

The sound of the front door.

"Sonofabitch!" Charley yelled, hurtling past Peter Vincent. He bounded down the steps, taking them three at a time. From the landing, he caught a fleeting glimpse of his prey.

As long taloned fingers slid gracefully around the door, closing it with a click.

It took maybe ten seconds to clear the bottom steps of the sprawling Billy-thing's oily remains. Another three to hit the door and fling it open, murder in his heart.

But by then it was gone.

"Damn!" Charley yelled. "Damn damn damn damn!"

Peter stood at the top of the stairs, staring down from the promenade. "Charley," he yelled, "get away from the door! It could be a trap!"

Charley almost wished it was. *Anything would beat this peekaboo bullshit,* he thought.

"Dandrige, show your face if you're so tough!" he called out.

Peter looked down at him like he'd just swallowed a turd. "Charley," he squeaked.

Charley had about had it. He whirled around like a teenaged Kali-cultist, waving his cross. *"DANDRIGE! C'mon out and kill me if you can!"*

"Charley, come *here*!" Peter cried, adamant.

"DANDRIGE IS A CHICKENSHIT DOUGHWAD! DANDRIGE IS A PENCIL-NECKED GEEK! DANDRIGE IS AFRAID OF HIS OWN SHAD—"

He was cut off in mid-epithet as every clock in the Dandrige house went off in ragged unison, a cacophony of tones and timbres, all pointing to one crucial fact. The time.

Six o'clock.

Charley stared up at Peter Vincent, smiling wickedly. Peter looked at him like the original stern father figure, was about to repeat *Charley, you get up here right this minute...*

... when the enormous stained-glass window behind him shattered inward, spraying him with a rainbow of glistening shards. He threw his arms up protectively and crouched down.

"Not nice," hissed the vampire, just a few feet away. *"Très, très gauche."*

Peter Vincent was slack-jawed with terror. It took considerably more will than he thought he had to even speak. His voice came out forced and brittle. "Charley, stay right there," he said. "I *mean* it."

Dandrige winked at him patronizingly. "So," he crooned, "just the two of us, eh? Real man-to-man stuff. I like that." He nudged conspiratorially, circling for the kill.

Peter pulled his cross out reflexively, holding it at arm's length. Dandrige smiled a long smile. "I told you before. You have to have faith for that, you pathetic. Old. Man.

"Let me tell you something about my kind," he continued, his voice cutting the air like a razor. "You'll no doubt find this information utterly absorbing. We kill for three reasons: for food, for spawn and for sport.

"The latter is decidedly the most painful.

"*Your* way, Mr. Vincent."

Dandrige moved in, closer and closer, his words simultaneously degrading and hypnotic. The world seemed to close in around Peter as the vampire spoke, blinding him to everything but his words, his mouth.

His teeth.

And then, just as he was about to slip over the edge, he saw it. And the cognizance of it brought him back, made him whole again.

Seeing it made him think the whole affair very, very funny.

He wanted Dandrige to see it, too.

Dandrige felt something go subtly askew. One moment, the old fart was putty in his hands; the next, he was awake, aware...

... and *smiling*.

Peter Vincent beamed like an only child on Christmas morning. The cross seemed to grow heavier in his hands. He let it drop slightly, clearing his throat.

"Mr. Dandrige," he said. "I have learned several things of inestimable value this night. First, that you are above all else an insufferable ass; and second," he winked, "even a *pathetic old man* can have his day.

"Look over your shoulder."

Dandrige turned with mounting horror to see the first pink tendrils of dawn breaking over the neighboring rooftops. He let out a little primal screech, then whirled to face Peter Vincent. Peter held up the cross, the tiniest scintilla of dawn *pinging* off it like red-hot needles firing straight into Dandrige's eyes.

"*Nooo...*" he hissed, and broke away. He ran to the stairs to find Charley at the bottom, *his* cross another impenetrable obstacle.

"Got him!" Charley cried.

And then they heard the shrieking, clawing sound coming down the hall.

From the attic.

"Amy..." said Charley, faltering. Showing an instant of indecision.

In that instant, Dandrige leapt.

Twenty-Seven

By his own admission, Charley had experienced close to three thousand four hundred hours of cinematic horror and mayhem in his brief life. He had seen giant carnivorous rabbits, twelve-year-olds in the throes of demonic possession, dogs split open and spewing the tendrils of alien hosts, an endless parade of vampires, psychos and blood-sucking freaks. He had seen special effects that ranged from the insanely laughable to the mind-bendingly authentic.

He had seen nothing to prepare him for the sight of Jerry Dandrige diving headfirst toward him and *mutating* on the way: arms twisting and stretching into wings, incredibly huge, eight feet if they were an inch; legs stunting in mid-fall, shriveling into tiny hooked appendages; body bristling even as it shrank.

And his face...

... his face was the worst. It led the charge, mouth gaping and screeching, down and down.

Charley ducked at the last moment, and the bat-thing snatched at him, coming away with a bleeding divot of scalp. Charley screamed and clutched his head. The bat-thing arched high toward the vaulted ceiling, turned, swooped again...

... and ran straight into Peter Vincent, coming down the stairs. It bowled him over, attaching itself to his neck viciously, all teeth and tiny claws and furious beating wings.

They fell to the floor in a heap, Peter fighting the onslaught desperately, the creature tearing at him and trying to secure a killing hold. Charley raced forward, grabbing it roughly by the wings...

... and the bat-thing lashed out, jaws snapping, and fastened itself to his hand, shaking it like a pit bull shakes a rat, the blood spurting hot and black. Charley fell back with a howl, and the bat-thing turned back to Peter Vincent, pausing only once to arc its head back...

... and *laugh*, an insane, impossible cackle that burst from its tiny lungs as the nightmare visage turned back on the prostrate form beneath it, eyes shiny and mad with blood-lust...

... utterly unaware of the soft, bright beams of morning sun that inched down the stairs...

... the killing sun...

Charley looked up in pain to find Peter on his last legs, unable to fight any longer. The bat-thing reared its head in triumph...

... and the first light of day hit it square in the head.

Its scream was a hideous, bleating thing. It pulled its head away, one side crisping under the prolonged exposure. It jerked away from Peter Vincent and careened down the hall toward the basement, knocking over furniture and knickknacks as it went. A thick, acrid plume of smoke trailed after it.

It smelled of dead things left too long in the sun.

Charley crawled over to Peter Vincent, who lay coughing in the warming sun. "My God, Peter, are you all right?" he asked. Peter nodded, bruised and scratched but miraculously unhurt.

They looked around, the sudden stillness entirely unnerving. Peter groaned. "Charley, help me up," he said. "We don't have much time."

Wounded and disheveled, they made their way toward the cellar door. Not knowing that something else made its way downward through a darkened rear stairwell.

Something changed.
Something growing.
Something very very hungry.

Twenty-Eight

They descended the stairs to the basement with roughly the same enthusiasm Dante reserved for the Inferno. The darkness was complete, the only visibility provided by Peter's flashlight. It cut swaths across the darkness, revealing a hodgepodge of musty furniture, all covered by heavy canvas dropcloths. Beyond them were what appeared to be four rather large windows covered with securely fastened blackout drapes.

And there were rats. The flashlight illuminated scuttling bodies darting in and out of the row of antiques, poking whiskered faces out of bookshelves and cubbyholes, indignant at the intrusion. Not a lot—no great hordes—but enough to preserve the aura of decay.

No coffin, though. After a dozen sweeps of the beam, Peter saw no sign of Dandrige. Or his coffin.

Charley stood beside him in the darkness, holding a kerchief to his scalp. The wound wasn't deep, thank God, but it had bled, and thin rivulets dried and caked on his cheeks.

They glanced at each other, and without a word began ripping the dust covers from the furniture. They found several mirrors (evidently removed from pieces of furniture upstairs), a rather imposing chest of drawers, an armoire and several pieces worthy of Sotheby's.

But no coffin.

Then Peter noticed the rats. Rats everywhere, but a concentration of them seemed to favor the armoire. He dropped down to the floor, training his flashlight underneath.

His eyes bulged wide in his head.

"Charley, help me move this thing!" They grabbed matter-of-factly and h*eaved*...

... and the rats poured out in a flood, beady-eyed and bloated. Charley and Peter just stared, silently mouthing *Jesus Christ* in unison.

It was an alcove, tiny and oppressive. The stone walls were cold and mildewed. Another window, recently bricked up, adorned one wall *(probably hadn't had enough time to do the others*, Charley thought).

The rats were everywhere, hundreds of them, chittering and squawking at the intrusion. And two coffins: one ornate, hardwood, brass-bound; the other plain, little more than a large packing crate. Peter looked in the lesser, feeling the soil. There was something inside. Carefully he picked it up, shining his flashlight upon it. It was a jacket.

Amy's jacket.

Charley moaned at the sight of it. He'd almost forgotten her in the madness of the last few minutes. He threw a concerned look at Peter, whispering her name.

As if on cue, the stairs creaked. Charley started back through the darkness, toward the door. Peter called out, hoping to stop him.

No such luck. In an instant, the shadows swallowed him up. Peter rushed over to the coffin, grabbing the lid with shaking hands.

Only to find it resist. The clasps released all right, but some internal mechanism was evidently in place. So, he did what any vampire hunter worth his salt would do in such circumstances.

He picked the lock.

Charley picked his way carefully through the darkness; afraid of what he'd find, more afraid of not finding it.

It: the girl he loved, the once-and-future Mrs. Charles Brewster. He pressed on, his eyes slowly adjusting to the darkness. He couldn't stand it: the pain, the loss, the destruction of his car, his friends, his love life... his *whole* life. It was too much. It was unbearable. It was...

It was standing before him, calling his name.

"*Charleeee...*"

He recoiled instantly. Amy looked hurt. She brought her hands to her throat coquettishly. "Don't be afraid, Charley," she purred. "It's only me. Amy..." Her voice trailed off.

She advanced slowly, with a husky sensuality he'd never dared dream of. Her eyes burned into him, red-rimmed and horrible, yet somehow... soft. Yes, soft and wanting. *She wants me.* The thought appeared in his mind of its own volition, a palpable thing.

Amy smiled knowingly, unbuttoning her blouse as she spoke. Charley stared unbelievingly. She was naked underneath. She ran her hands from her belly to her breasts, an inviting, languorous gesture. "What's wrong, Charley? Don't you *want* me anymore?"

He did. He felt himself slipping, wanting to slide, to slide fully into her... need. She had changed; she was ripe fruit, dangled in front of a starving man. She smelled of sweet, fresh orchids. Her breasts were full and heavy, responding to her kneading, nipples hard as thimbles. Her belly was firm and quivering, her mons...

Amy took his hand gently and put it there, undulating her hips, a preview of coming attractions. Charley groaned and fell into her arms, pressing into her. *Nothing matters anymore. Nothing but this, forever and ever and...*

He opened his eyes to stare at his beloved. "Oh, Charley," she breathed. "I love yoooooou..." His vision blurred, started to fade. But not before he glimpsed himself in a mirror.

Standing with his arms wrapped around nothing, dry-humping the thin air before him.

Reality poured back into him like a bucket of icy sea water. He pushed away from her, thrusting his crucifix forward. She hissed like cold oil on a hot plate, burying her face in her hands.

"It's not *my* fault, Charley. You *promised* you wouldn't let him get me. You *promised*..."

She started to cry. Charley faltered, wracked with guilt. "Amy, I'm sorry," he whispered, dropping his guard.

And Amy whirled, teeth flashing, whipping one delicately clawed hand around to knock the cross spinning into the darkness. Charley never knew what hit him.

She dropped the thin veneer, advancing on him slowly, like a hungry wolf advances on a cornered buck. Sure of itself.

Sure of the kill.

"I know," she smiled. "But you'll do."

Peter Vincent heard the commotion, guessed what was happening. He prayed that Charley could hold out a few more minutes, until he got the coffin open. He glanced over at her coffin, a few feet away. In desperation, he leaned over and kicked it. It fell to the floor with a clatter, soil spilling everywhere.

A scream cut through the darkness, an animal shriek of fear and outrage.

Good, he thought.

The lock clicked open. Peter threw back the lid, stake in hand.

Dandrige lay in his coffin, not breathing, not moving. The entire left side of his face was a mass of seared flesh, the hair burned away, the eyelid drooping.

Preview of coming attractions, he thought, and brought the stake down hard...

... as the vampire's arm lashed out, catching the old man by the throat, its one good eye blazing with raw, primal hatred. The stake missed its mark, plowing into the vampire's shoulder as it sat up in the coffin, raising Peter several inches off the floor and *throwing* him...

Amy screamed like a cat in a burning cage, leaping at Charley. He fell back against one of the mirrors, smashing it to the floor, where it shattered into a million fragments. He landed hard and scrabbled backward like a crab, cutting himself over and over...

Peter Vincent landed in a choking heap upon the wreckage of Amy's coffin. Dandrige rose up, the portrait of a dark god, wreaking vengeance on the desecrating infidels. He pulled the stake from his shoulder and flung it, the tip still smoking, across the room.

Peter backed against the wall, mind racing. Dandrige scowled horribly.

"I've *had* it with you," the vampire spat. "You are dead meat, my friend." He stood directly over Peter, leaning over to pick him up...

... as Amy crawled up to Charley, his blood from a dozen tiny lacerations more than she could bear. She licked her lips like a dog in an Alpo commercial, thin trails of saliva pouring out the corners of her mouth.

Charley backed into a pile of dropcloths and scrambled up over them, until he was flush against the wall. He spread his hands out in either direction, as if hoping to flatten out entirely. Amy grasped his ankles, making horrible smacking sounds.

And his left hand found something soft.
Something thick.
The blackout curtain.

Dandrige grasped Peter roughly by the lapels. Peter grabbed blindly for anything: a weapon, a prayer...

And found both.

Dandrige yanked him straight up off the floor, mouth gaping, drawing him close...

... and Peter Vincent, The Great Vampire Killer, pushed a fourteen-inch sliver of packing crate squarely into his chest.

Dandrige stopped in mid-snarl, his one eye opened wide in shock and agony. Peter twisted out of his grasp. Dimly, the actor could see what was happening on the other side of the room.

Charley kicked at Amy's face, striking a glancing blow. She fell back, and Charley *pulled*...

The curtain split open with a rending sound, sending a narrow beam of light slicing through the darkness.

Right into Jerry Dandrige's back.

It hit the vampire like a freight train, slamming him against the stone wall and pinning him there, smoldering, a solid foot above the floor. He writhed like a slug under a magnifying glass, an endless keening wail issuing up from deep inside him. *"NOOOOOOO!!!"*

A cry echoed raucously by Amy, who watched in horror, her eyes turning milky and blind with terror. Charley lurched over, reaching behind her to grab another curtain. He pulled with both hands, the entire drape coming away this time, flooding the room with light. Charley grabbed the curtain as it fell, throwing it over Amy protectively. She curled into a fetal position under it, her cries muffled by the heavy fabric.

The light hit the shattered fragments of glass, sending countless refractions firing in every direction, spidery beams of cleansing color and light.

"Got you, mother-*fucker!*" cried Charley, staring at Dandrige victoriously.

The vampire cast him one final, baleful look. Seeing only his own death.

Seeing nothing.

Then—before Charley, Peter and God Almighty—Dandrige began to burn.

It didn't take long. He seemed to fill with light: a clear, greenish glow that started deep inside, at his very core. It filled him until it seemed he might burst, puffing his torso out, stretching his limbs tight, rigid in agony.

Then it flooded out of his pores: brilliant fiery needles of light pushing out and out, intertwining with the countless prisms reflecting from the basement floor.

And he was molten, and he was charred, and he was ash, all in the space of a minute. All pinned to the alcove wall.

And he was awake through it all: awake, and aware.

His screams died like a candle being snuffed.

And it was over.

Peter and Charley lay in opposite corners of the room, sweating and panting and staring at one another in triumphant disbelief, as might the two sole survivors of a jet crash. Their gaze turned to the bundle of blackout drapery. Charley approached it, afraid to look under it.

Afraid not to.

He lifted it gingerly. Peter stared at him, covered in the thick gray ash that had been Jerry Dandrige, and waited. Charley looked up at him, his expression inscrutable, utterly drained.

"Peter," he said. "Call an ambulance."

Epilogue

Cookie Puss was back. Sometimes it seemed like Cookie Puss never really went away. There were nights where Charley woke up screaming, not with the pictures of Dandrige and Billy and Amy, but with the voice of Tom Carvel loudly croaking in his ears.

He lay back on his bed, a pile of pillows behind him, his shirt wide open and his pants undone. His many lacerations were pretty well healed over, although most of them had left scars that would never quite go away. For that, and for other reasons, he tended to like his clothing loose around him now.

Laying there, as he often did, made him think of the night when it had all begun: of godforsaken bra clasps and frustrated embraces, of Amy holding back while he plunged headlong. The sight of coffins being toted in the moonlight still lingered, of course; but it was little virginal Amy Peterson that he thought of most often, and her reluctant but firm resistance to his ardor.

It was something he would never know again.

The toad-voiced ice-cream vendor and his wares disappeared, thank God, from the screen. They were replaced, no thanks to God, by the bellowing pinheads from Barney's Karpet Kingdom. Late-night television, Charley was convinced, went on in a permanent time warp. The constant flux of life and death notwithstanding, Barney's would continue to sell carpets cheaper, every five minutes, on Channel 13.

He closed his eyes, and let himself slide back to the night of the end...

The aftermath had been nearly as lunatic as the events leading up to it. Somehow, he and Peter had managed to get Amy to the Brewster house, where the ambulance was to pick them up. Exposure to the sun didn't seem to make her any worse, or any better. And neither he nor Peter were in the greatest shape themselves.

They had forgotten entirely about Evil Ed. It hurt to think about it, sometimes: how his erstwhile friend had died so horribly, then slipped so readily from virtually everyone's mind. Charley hadn't even known about it; there hadn't been much time to discuss it at the time.

Mrs. Brewster had come home to an open door, a broken banister, a demolished table of knickknacks and a boneless pool of goop under the stairs. She had quite naturally called the police, not knowing that her son was already in something like custody.

And the questions! Oh, the questions! They gave no indication of ever coming to an end. Kindly old Lieutenant Detective Lennox had gone well out of his way to make the hours that followed as cheerful as possible. The famous vampire-hunting prowess of Peter Vincent had impressed him very little.

Seven hours later, when the police had finally and reluctantly allowed them to leave, they'd gotten back to the hospital just in time to discover Amy's fate.

He opened his eyes at the sound of the *Fright Night* theme music: Bach's ever-popular *Toccata and Fugue in D Minor*. The familiar drippy blood-red logo was draped over the familiar clips of Karloff, Lugosi, two generations of Chaneys.

Followed by the same old cheesy cemetery set.
Followed by the show's terrific new host.

After Peter was fired, one of the wiseass stagehands had taken a shot at ghost-hosting. Within three days, half the teenage population of Rancho Corvallis had risen in protest. The station managers had been boggled by the response. The stagehand had gone back to wisecracking from the shadows.

The new host stood a good bit taller than the old Peter Vincent. Despite the neck brace, he was a far more formidable presence. The utter confidence that had shown through, in all those old movies, was back.

"Good evening," Peter camped in grand old fashion, "and welcome to *Fright Night*. Tonight's grisly thriller takes you, not beyond the grave, but beyond the stars, as John Agar and Leo G. Carroll defend the earth from alien monsters in *Mars Wants Flesh...* !"

"Honey?" Charley's mom called, rapping gently on the door. Charley jumped, just a little, and the figure beside him stirred.

"What is it, Mom?" he answered, zipping his pants with his one free hand. He didn't think that she'd come in, but you could never tell.

"Just going to bed now, sweetie. Thank God for Valium." He heard her try to stifle an enormous yawn, then giggle. "Good night, dears!"

"G'night, Mom."

"G'night, Mrs. Brewster," called a third voice, sleepily, from beside him.

It had been touch and go there for a while. Aside from the massive blood loss and the million lacerations (not the least of which were the two holes in her neck), she'd also been clubbed over the back of the head and hurled through a window. She'd made a reasonably speedy recovery; but even now, nearly three months later, she had a couple of spots that he was careful not to touch.

Only a couple. Very easily gotten around.

Amy sighed and curled around him. He sighed and held her tight. Her blouse was open, and the greatly enhanced cleavage that Jerry Dandrige had given her pressed sweetly against his naked chest. *The one good thing that came of this*, he thought happily.

He'd skillfully removed her bra three hours ago, having mastered the art in the last few weeks of practice. They'd made love twice tonight, in fact; and from the way she was looking at him, the odds were good that they were about to do it again...

"Oh, Charley!" his mother interrupted again, this time from down the hall. "Did you notice that there are lights on in the house next door again? I swear, I don't understand why people wait until the middle of the night to move! You'd think they'd be *exhausted* by the time they..."

"*Damn,*" Charley quietly hissed. Amy rolled her eyes and shrugged her shoulders. He gave her a little peck on the forehead, then dragged himself to his feet and moved to the window.

Directly across the way, in what had once been Dandrige's bedroom window, a pair of baleful red eyes stared out at him.

"No," he moaned, heart jackhammering in his chest, as the glowing red lights blinked once, twice. Amy jumped up from the bed and moved quickly to his side...

... as the lights blinked again, then veered sharply to the left and disappeared...

... as the U-Haul trailer backed hesitantly into the driveway, taillights blinking one last time and then cutting out completely. A harmless-looking middle-aged man in chinos and a jean jacket got out of the car. His equally harmless-looking family could be seen through the living room window.

Amy breathed a sigh of relief and held Charley tight. "You had me scared for a minute there." She nuzzled his neck. "Now, *please*, come back to bed."

Charley stood, rigid and uncertain, staring at the window that faced his own. The ghost of a woman's scream echoed faintly in his mind. "I'm not so sure, baby," he ventured hesitantly. "I mean, what if something is still knocking around in there? What if...?"

Amy opened her blouse, and brushed her bare breasts against his shoulder blades.

"Then you'll deal with it, lover." She smiled. "In the meantime, deal with this."

Charley groaned and turned to her. *It was just the trailer lights,* he told himself. *Of course it was.*

But what if...?

Then Amy did something extra-specially nice, and the question became instantly moot. *Then you'll deal with it, lover*, she'd said, with utter confidence.

And if it came down to it, he would.

"Right," he whispered, reaching back casually to draw the blinds.

And the two of them went back to bed.

JOHN SKIPP

A *New York Times* bestselling writer, editor, social critic, splatterpunk poster child, literary zombie champion, and all-around horror legend. His books include *The Light at the End, The Cleanup, The Scream, Deadlines, The Bridge, Animals, Fright Night, Book of the Dead*, and *Still Dead* (with Craig Spector); *The Emerald Burrito of Oz* (with Marc Levinthal); *Jake's Wake, The Day Before*, and *Spore* (with Cody Goodfellow); *Opposite Sex* (as Gina McQueen); *Conscience, Stupography*, and *The Long Last Call* (solo); and, as solo editor, *Mondo Zombie, Zombies: Encounters with the Hungry Dead*, and *Werewolves and Shapeshifters: Encounters With the Beast Within*.

He is also sometimes guest fiction editor of *The Magazine of Bizarro Fiction*, and has a long-standing passion for music and film. He lives with family and friends, both human and otherwise, on a hill overlooking the glistening spires of downtown Los Angeles.

www.johnskipp.com

CRAIG SPECTOR

An award-winning and bestselling author and screenwriter, with 12 books published, reprints in 9 languages, and millions of copies in print. His fiction has been published by Tor/St. Martin's Press, Bantam Books, Harper Collins, Pocket Books, Arbor House and others; his film and television work includes projects for TNC Pictures, ABC, NBC, Fox, Hearst Entertainment, Davis Entertainment Television, New Line Cinema, Beacon Pictures, and Disney. An accomplished musician and graduate of the Berklee College of Music [1982], Spector has a new music album released in 2017, charting his journey fighting prostate cancer, metastasized to his bones.

www. craigspector.com